THE COCAINE AUDIT

D1602818

a novel by

Jonathan van der Borgh

The Cocaine Audit

Copyright © 2013 Jonathan van der Borgh

Chapter 1

1

My mother and father were complete opposites. Maybe that's why their marriage worked so well, but whatever the reason they were devoted to each other.

My father William Verity was quintessentially English. He was tall with pale blue eyes and had a small clipped moustache and thinning mousy hair. He stood bolt upright and walked with a military gait. He was an economist in charge of the risk analysis department of a multi-national oil company. His greatest passion, except for my mother of course, was cricket. He'd got his blue for cricket when he was up at Cambridge where he studied Economics and got a first class degree. He viewed the whole of life as if it were a game of cricket which made him rather eccentric. Many of his expressions were cricketing terms.

"Well played!" he would say, on hearing of some piece of good news. It was important in life to "keep your eye on the ball" and whatever the vicissitudes thrown at you you had to "play a straight bat". Crossing the road in his company was a challenging affair. He pushed forward at an imaginary ball with his rolled umbrella. "Come one" he would cry as he darted across the street between the passing traffic, expecting you to follow. My mother would remain frozen to the pavement and wait until the coast was clear before crossing sedately to the other side. I have often wondered how many people my father ran out during his cricketing career.

My mother Evgenia Polunin was a Russian ballerina from St Petersburg. As a girl she had been picked out from the crowd of hopeful swans by her teacher and had been groomed for stardom. There followed years of hard work and physical strain. She once told me that the programme of academic subjects was just as tough as the dancing regime. She studied three languages at ballet school, Russian, French and English, in addition to mathematics and statistics and history.

Evgenia had been one of the lead dancers in the first visit of the Kirov to London since the end of the cold war. Fate plays funny little tricks in life and she had sprained her ankle badly during the tour so that she was unable to dance for the last week or two. Hugh Templeman, one of the Trustees of Covent Garden was also a member of the MCC and he suggested that she might enjoy spending a day at Lord's Cricket Ground. It would be pleasant to sit in the open air and relax by watching the game, rather than traipsing around an art gallery or a stuffy old museum.

As you've already guessed she met my father at Lord's. He was enchanted by her. She was very dark-haired and exotic and spoke English with a thick Russian accent. Hugh Templeman had to go back to the city for a board meeting so he left Bill in charge of Evgenia.

Bill was surprised and delighted that Evgenia was not only quick to pick up the rudiments of the game but also seemed to enjoy it. He was equally delighted by her occasional misuse of English.

"Oh Beel", she said "the wicked keeper is so athletic, he is so clever with his balls, he would make a wonderful ballet dancer. How the chorus would love him".

And how he would love the chorus, thought Bill, knowing of the wicket keeper's predilection for attractive young women.

Later, over lunch, Evgenia told Bill about her visit to the Templemans for supper the previous evening. Mary Templeman was famous for her cooking and also for her large collection of budgerigars which she had been breeding for many years.

"Mary Templeman showed me her ovary", said Evgenia "it has such pretty coloured eggs in it". Bill tried not to show his surprise at this startling piece of information.

By the time they had finished lunch my father had decided that he wanted to spend the rest of his life with Evgenia. He hit on a cunning plan. He would ask Evgenia if she would like to spend the week-end in Cambridge, they would stay with his married sister Georgina for propriety's sake. Cambridge would look stunning at this time of year with the different shades of green leaves on the trees and the Backs would be a romantic place to woo Evgenia. They could go punting on the Cam and he would be able to show her all the old haunts which he knew and loved so well. It was the long vacation so there would only be a few undergraduates around, otherwise the place would be empty.

To his relief Evgenia jumped at the idea so Bill went into the Pavilion and phoned Georgina who naturally agreed to the proposal, in fact she was most intrigued at the fact that Bill seemed to be rather smitten with this Russian ballerina and couldn't wait to meet her. Georgina's husband Simon Hartridge was professor of Botany at Cambridge University and was always very welcoming. He had created a superb walled garden with a heated greenhouse where he grew exotic plants which he collected when he and Georgina travelled overseas.

Bill and Evgenia travelled up to Cambridge by car on the Friday evening and arrived in time for a light supper. Evgenia and Georgina hit it off immediately and went into a huddle while Simon told Bill all about their recent trip to Turkey where he'd been plant-hunting. After a stroll in the garden in the moonlight they retired to their separate rooms for the night. Next morning over breakfast they announced to Georgina and Simon that they were engaged to be married.

2

Years later my aunt Georgina told me what had happened. Evgenia had told her the whole story.

Bill had been lying in bed unable to sleep whilst fantasizing about what Evgenia would look like with no clothes on. Suddenly he heard his door being stealthily opened and closed and Evgenia stood beside his bed in her nightdress. It was a very bright moonlit night. She looked him right in the eye and undid the top button of her nightie. It fell to the floor revealing her stark naked except for the bandage around her injured ankle. She slipped into bed beside him.

Bill slowly unwound the bandage from her ankle and kissed it "to make it better" said Evgenia with a glint in her eye. The kissing spread to other more intimate regions and they ended up entwined around each other, spending all night together.

"I wanted to know how we would be together in bed" said Evgenia to Georgina "before I agreed to marry Beel. I just knew he was going to ask me".

"It must have been alright then?" enquired Georgina.

"Oh yes," said Evgenia, going slightly pink at the memory "Beel was like a rotting stag", and then, very quietly as she remembered more "but so gentle with me".

3

Bill and Effie were married at Cambridge Registry Office by special licence with Simon and Geogina as witnesses, and the Templemans as the only guests. It was a lovely summer's day and after the brief ceremony they all went back to Simon and Georgina's house for a wedding breakfast on the terrace in the shade of the vine which grew on an overhead trellis.

They travelled to St Petersburg for the honeymoon. Bill had no pre-conceived ideas about St Petersburg and he was surprised at what a simply beautiful city it is. Effie introduced him to her family, a large, emotional, boisterous collection of Russians who immediately embraced their new in-law.

Bill decided to try to learn Russian and in his methodical way he worked out a plan of how to get a quick grasp of the new language. He started out by learning the parts of the body, then common objects. After learning the nouns Bill could soon put sentences together and get attuned to the sounds and with his prodigious and well-trained memory he was able to recall pretty well all the words he had spoken. Later he would get a grip on the written word but for now it was enough to be able to carry on a conversation with anyone he met.

Effie was very proud of Bill's effort to speak her native tongue. As they strolled together on Nevsky Prospekt and along the banks of the Neva River, Effie taught Bill how to make love to someone in Russian, and she corrected his mistakes and his pronounciation of difficult words. But Bill never corrected her English.

They travelled south to Moscow and stayed in a dacha belonging to one of Effie's cousins in the countryside outside the city. They walked in the forest and lay side by side in the sweet-smelling grass looking up through the trees at the huge Russian sky. Their holiday came to an end and they travelled back to London to start a new life together. Bill went back to work in his oil company, he'd been newly promoted to head-up the green energy department and evaluate potential investments in sustainable forms of power generation, and Effie got a part-time job teaching ballet.

They lived in Bill's house in Cadogan Street in Chelsea which Bill had inherited when his parents had died.

Effie made a few alterations to the decor of the house and introduced some Russian furniture and pictures, but otherwise it remained the same rather lovely, untidy home with a lived-in feel about it and books and pictures everywhere. "'Cultured chaos' my Mother described it", said Bill.

And it was in this very house that I made my first appearance into this world precisely nine months to the day after Bill and Effie were married.

4

I was an only child. I don't know whether my mother could not have any more children or whether she just didn't want to have any more children, but whatever the cause I was an only child and as a result I was the centre of my parents' attention and treated as an adult from an early age. I am also completely bilingual because my mother always spoke to me in Russian and my father in English which means of course that I can read both English and Russian literature in their original languages. Every year we went to Russia for at least one of our holidays so that I became immersed in all things Russian and appreciated its history and culture and I got to know all my Russian cousins and uncles and aunts.

As soon as I was old enough my parents took me to the ballet and to the theatre and concerts, and we usually went to an art gallery or a museum at least a couple of times a month. I could read and write by the time I was four and a half years old and I suppose I might have become rather precocious except that my father was very fond of the outdoor life so that as often as possible we used to go on camping trips to each of the British National Parks in turn and this meant long walks in different types of terrain. My parents refused to carry me so that I had to plod along on my own two legs even when very young. My father was also keen on bird-watching and my mother had an extraordinary knowledge of wild flowers and all of this rubbed off on me.

We had an allotment at Ascot Allotments in Ealing and every week we went to our plot either by tube, or by car if we needed to transport more stuff than we could carry. We worked away at our vegetable growing and my mother's Russian upbringing meant that we grew masses of beetroots and onions and cabbages and celery so that she could make soups to remind her of her childhood. They tasted wonderful. We got to know most of the other folk at the allotments, they were a mixed crowd and very supportive to each other and would lend tools and equipment and exchange seeds and plants freely.

Pretty well every allotment had a shed and we also had a small greenhouse, so that we were able to grow tomatoes and peppers and cucumbers and aubergines. There's nothing quite like the satisfaction of eating a ripe tomato which you've grown yourself. My mother struck up a friendship with a Mrs Grodzinski who came from a family of Polish bakers. She and Effie would reminisce about their childhood under the Soviets and share sandwiches made of heavy black bread with garlic sausage. Mrs Grodzinski kept a few hens on her allotment which meant she had to come every day to feed and water them and to collect any eggs and she would water our plants as well as her own when necessary.

Every year in the autumn at harvest time we had a big party at the allotments and we all contributed and cooked and ate a variety of vegetables and home-made sauces with barbecued sausages and other meats. There was plenty of wine and beer and cider and we weaved our way home replete and happy.

5

The only serious difference of opinion I can ever remember my parents had was over my schooling. My father wanted me to go to his old private boarding schools in the country but my mother was obdurate.

"Private schools are for the parents. They boast about where their children are at school. The children grow up with such a narrow view and with such boring friends. I want Tommy to know everybody of all types. And besides why would we want him to be away from us and to be brought up by complete stranglers?"

In the end my father gave in and I went first of all to Bousfield Primary School in Bolton Gardens and then on to Holland Park School in Airlie Gardens. The teaching in both schools was pretty good and one or two members of staff were inspirational, especially the French teacher at Bousfield Primary and the maths teacher at Holland Park. Also, I made crowds of friends and got involved with plenty of after-school activities.

Much to my father's dismay I was hopeless at ball games but the school had a link with the Thames Rowing Club at Putney and because I grew big and strong for my age I was encouraged to become a junior member at Thames and spent all the games periods as well as hours of my own free time on the river. Most of all I enjoyed the early morning training sessions when the sun was just coming up and there was mist over the water and few people around except the odd dog walker or cyclist on the tow path and water birds in the reeds and flying overhead. And home for a full English breakfast.

In the sixth form at Holland Park I took maths, physics, French and Russian. During my last year at school I went on a trek with a school party to the Nepalese Himalaya where we walked the Jomsom trail. The first view of Annapurna is quite a shock, no photograph can prepare you for the enormity of the mountain. The junior eight at Thames Rowing Club also rowed at Henley Regatta which was fun but we didn't get any further than the second round and a repêcharge. Thanks to the teaching and a good peer group I got A* in all subjects so I could pretty well choose the university I wanted to go to, and in the end I accepted a scholarship to Imperial College to read maths.

6

After a few weeks at Imperial I was sitting at a table in the cafeteria during a coffee break with a friend who'd been at school with me when we were joined by a girl who sat down and introduced herself.

"My name's Petronella Kovacs" she said "but everybody calls me Polly". She was so beautiful that my pal and I just stared at her. She was dark haired with amazing dark brown eyes and wonderful olive skin, and she was wearing a brightly coloured silk scarf round her neck which contrasted with her brown woollen sweater and brown corduroy jeans. She looked just like a gypsy which it turned out wasn't very far from the truth as her family had come to England from Romania, and had settled in Whitechapel which is where she and her two brothers had been born and brought up.

I recovered myself and said "I'm Tom Verity and this is Charlie Boswell, we were at school together".

Charlie said "Hi!" and then gathered up his books and shuffled off to his next lecture. He was reading physics. I was free for the rest of the day so I sat talking to Polly. She turned out to be very bright and was reading statistics which meant that we would be going to a number of the same lectures and that our courses overlapped in several areas. I found it very easy to talk to Polly, she was interested in so many different subjects and was obviously a free spirit and was completely unselfconscious.

After a while she looked at her watch.

"Goodness, is it that late?" she said, "I must fly".

"How would you like to have some dinner one evening?" I asked involuntarily. I waited for her to decline the offer, she must have masses of boy friends, possibly a special one.

"I'd love to", said Polly "let's go to the Bocca di Leoni for some pasta. Then we might take in a film?....... tomorrow would be good, what time?"

And so we met outside the Science Museum at seven o'clock the following evening and strolled through the side streets under the London plane trees until we reached the restaurant. We sat inside at one of the tables in a stall surrounded on three sides by a wooden barrier. The food was delicious and we sipped a glass of the house red. I can remember feeling completely at ease as we chatted about our lives and told each other about our families and childhood. After we'd drunk our coffee it seemed the most natural thing in the world to put my arm around Polly's shoulders and to kiss her.

Now I had kissed a few girls in my time but this was quite different. It wasn't just a question of lips meeting lips, it consumed my whole body, so that my throat felt constricted and my stomach tightened and my breathing became shallow.

"I had started to think there was something wrong with me", said Polly, "you're the first man who's kissed me since I started at Imperial". She took my hand and held it palm upwards tracing my life line with the nail on her index finger. Then as if she had satisfied herself about something she drew my hand downwards and held it firmly on her thigh. She looked at me expectantly.

"Let's skip the film", I said "and I'll walk you home".

7

Polly lived in a garret under the eaves of a house near the Albert Hall. Lying in bed you could just see the tops of the trees in Hyde Park and hear the muffled sound of the traffic and the odd motor horn or bicycle bell. Other people's lives, I thought.

But my own life had taken an unexpected and wonderful turning. Next morning I lay on my back and recalled the previous night's passion. Softness, gentleness, urgency, satisfaction, all these but something more, something different, something indefinable, a kind of heart-rending tenderness. Could this be the real thing?

Later, after we'd showered, we sat wrapped in our bath towels and drank black coffee and ate white bread rolls with unsalted butter and black cherry jam for breakfast.

The flat was tiny but full of interest. Polly had a collection of photographic portraits covering the whole of one wall, so close together that they looked like a collage.

"Do you know who they are?" asked Polly.

"Tell me", I replied.

"They're the greatest mathematicians who've ever lived", she said, then "they're not the dry and dusty old individuals who most people imagine them to be, they were all exceptional in their own way and they led unexpected lives and shared the same feelings and emotions that we have". Then she took me on a tour of the gallery.

The first portrait was a woodcutting of Pythagoras. Naturally, from my own knowledge of maths I knew about his theorem and the fact that he had invented the idea that every number can be expressed either as a whole number or as a ratio using two numbers or integers, but I was completely ignorant of what sort of life he'd led.

"Pythagoras was born in 569 BC on the Greek island of Samos", said Polly "and travelled to Egypt where he was influenced by their philosophies and customs and was then taken as a prisoner of war to Babylon where he learned maths and music and science. Afterwards he went back to Samos and on to Croton in southern Italy. He founded his famous sect called mathematikoi which had strict rules – they all had to give up their possessions, become vegetarians and follow Pythagoras's rules. He thought that maths and philosophy and religion were all intertwined".

"Do you know what Pythagoras said?" asked Polly "he said 'Everything is Number'. When I heard that and realised its significance I decided to become a mathematician myself!"

"But why have you got a portrait of Buddha next to Pythagoras?" I asked.

"Well, Buddha - or Siddhartha Gautama as he was named when he was born just six years before Pythagoras – devised a way of describing the smallest particle or atom by using the number 7. His calculation worked out at 141.6 picometers which amazingly works out at about the same size as a carbon atom. Not bad for two and a half thousand years ago before anyone even knew that atoms existed".

Polly spent the next hour or so describing the lives and achievements of the rest of the subjects in her gallery, including Fermat, the Bernoulli family, Newton, Galileo, Turing, Einstein, Blaise Pascal, Fibonacci and Babbage. All just names to me before now but brought to life by Polly's enthusiasm and descriptions.

On the wall opposite the portrait gallery there were four large diagrams, drawn on cartridge paper in black ink and coloured with acrylic paints by Polly. She led me over to them.

"These four images are all well-known. The first picture is Florence Nightingale's famous diagram which she called 'of the causes of mortality in the army in the east'. Florence drew a coxcomb plot which you can see divided a circle into twelve parts, one for each month of the year".

"The area of the circle segments was scaled, with different colours to represent the numbers of soldiers dying from wounds sustained in battle, or from preventable disease, or from other factors in the Crimea. She used the diagram to persuade the War Office that by far the largest killer was disease, which could be controlled quite well even in the 1850s with simple measures of hygiene and care".

We moved to the second diagram.

"This was drawn in 1861 by a guy called Minard and illustrates the advance and retreat of Napoleon's army in Russia from 1812 to 1813" said Polly "You can see that the thickness of the line indicates the size of the army. From left to right the thick line on top shows the army travelling east, crossing the Neman River with 422,000 men, advancing into Russian territory and stopping in Moscow with only 100,000 men".

Polly pointed at the line and went on "then from right to left, the lower line shows the army returning west, including the disasterous crossing of the Berezina River. Only a small fraction of Napoleon's army, roughly 20,000 men, survived. The lower part of the graph gives the temperature during the army's retreat, in degrees below freezing on the Réaumur scale. It's all there in one picture".

I recognised the third diagram as the periodic table, which organises the one hundred and eighteen known chemical elements by selected properties of their atomic structure. They're shown in the periodic table by the increasing values of their atomic numbers, or in other words the number of protons in their atomic nuclei.

Polly explained that although the diagram is rectangular, there are counter-intuitive gaps in the horizontal rows or periods, so as to keep elements with similar properties together in each vertical column or group - such as the alkali metals, the alkali earths, the halogens, and the noble gases.

Lots of people in the past had tried to organise a periodic table, but it was an elderly Russian professor called Dmitri Mendeleyev in 1869 who actually fell asleep whilst puzzling over the problem and saw in a dream a table where all the elements fell into place as required like a pack of cards. When he woke up he immediately wrote it down on a piece of paper. And it has stood to this day.

The fourth and last diagram was a fantastic picture made up of weird shapes with bright colours and strange outlines and seemingly endless boundaries all different and irregular, yet somehow cohesive and altogether mesmerising.

"It's a Mandelbrot 'set'", said Polly "it's based on a mathematical formula developed by Benoit Mandelbrot to try and measure the edges of clouds or coastlines, or any other irregular shape or outline. The maths is horrendously difficult, but Mandelbrot invented a new item called a fractal which has now become a standard for this sort of stuff"

"All four diagrams have an immediate visual impact", Polly went on, "no table or list of numbers however cleverly compiled could ever grab someone's attention as vividly as these diagrams".

She paused.

"What I want to try to do is use visual aids like these - all based on accurate statistics of course – to help people to make the right decisions for their businesses or departments or ministries or sports clubs or whatever it is they're involved in. There now, you're the only person I've ever told about my ambitions".

"How will you start?", I asked.

"I already have", she said and moving over to her desk she switched on her iMac computer. The screen lit up at once and I noticed that her screen saver was a Mandelbrot Set which kept changing and revolving. Polly opened a folder and clicked on the first item inside it. A familiar image filled the screen. It was the map of the London Underground. Along all the lines there were dozens of dots which moved every now and then.

"The dots are trains in real time" explained Polly. "All this information is freely available on the web but only in tabular form, so I've created this diagram. You can see where every train is and where there are bottlenecks. It would be especially useful if there was an emergency like a fire or a terrorist attack, you could see at a glance how many trains were in the danger zone. If you enlarge the screen you can see that each train is identified by its individual number".

She closed down the map and opened another file.

"Here's the same thing for Network Rail. This shows every train and differentiates between goods trains and passenger trains. It also shows who the operator is as well as the identity of the engine. I can do the same thing for the motorways for the police and the rescue services. The information is all available on cameras".

Polly opened yet another file.

"Here's a plan of the EDF electricity network. The blue lines are the electricity being distributed to customers, the thickness of the line shows the volume of power being used. If there's a cut in supply for any reason you can see immediately where the fault lies and if it's posssible to re-route electricity to customers who've lost their supply. This can be done for all the electricity companies and globally as well".

"I'm in the middle of developing a plan for the water companies, with an overview of the whole country. This will show where supplies are low or there are leaks or other problems, it'll also show in real time where most of the water is being used".

Polly closed all the files and switched off her computer. She looked up at me. She'd been concentrating so hard on her screen and her explanations that she hadn't noticed that her bath towel had slipped off and that she was sitting completely naked on her stool. She could tell I'd been staring at her.

"What are you looking at, pervert?" she asked. I didn't say anything. She stood up and took me by the hand and led me back into the bedroom.

Chapter 2

1

Looking back at my time at Imperial College is like looking into a kaleidoscope of images. Polly is in the centre of these of course, but others come into focus if I concentrate.

Days on the river rowing in the engine room of the Imperial College second eight and the cameraderie of the other oarsmen;

Attending lectures in the Great Hall from visiting professors;

Camping in the Welsh mountains with Polly and walking in Snowdonia;

Drinking yards of ale with friends at the Chaps Club in the School of Mines;

Skiing in the Austrian Alps with the Imperial College ski club;

Discovering Tom Lehrer and Shelley Berman and Victor Borge;

A particular holiday in Russia with Bill and Effie and the joy of reading Tolstoy and Chekhov in the original Russian and of visiting Yasnaya Polyana and Yalta;

Working hard up in my freezing cold room and drinking scalding hot tea to keep me awake before my finals, I'd transferred to the Economics Faculty after my first year;

A walking holiday with Polly in the Italian Dolomites, staying in a succession of mountain huts;

Being persuaded by a scout from KPMG to train to become an accountant after I left Imperial College;

Wearing a gown and mortarboard when I graduated and Effie taking photographs and my parents being so proud of me although I only managed a 2:1;

Polly looking great at her graduation when she went up to receive her First and the prize for top student in her year;

Feeling rather flat after I came down from Imperial College and not at all sure if I really wanted to be an accountant after all;

Polly boosting me up and telling me not to be such a wet and in the next breath that she'd accepted a job at The Office for National Statistics.

2

There were twenty-three trainees in my year at KPMG. We came from a mixed background and the only thing we had in common was that we had all achieved at least a 2:1 in our degrees at university. From the first day it was made clear to us that we were very privileged to be part of the year's intake at KPMG and that we would be put under remorseless pressure for the duration of our contracts.

Trainees we were and trained we would be. All our training was to be in-house. Not for us the luxury of attending courses run by accountancy colleges or cramming institutions, oh no. We would be placed in different sections of the firm for a limited time each and our overseers would make detailed reports of our progress. We would attend in-house training sessions and would do our homework on time. There would be regular tests under examination conditions and anyone whose marks fell below a pre-ordained standard would be asked to leave. In the event only seven of us lasted the three year course. I hated every minute of it. But my goodness by the time I qualified I really knew my stuff. And that was the whole point.

For three years I had practically no free time. We spent weeks away from home in every part of the country, servicing clients which were engaged in almost every kind of business. The two main departments in the firm were audit and tax and this was the bread and butter of the organisation, but the jam came from hefty consultancy fees.

The most rewarding division to work in from my point of view was Business Recovery. It was here that one learnt that most businesses which go wrong do so because the managers realise too late that it's all over. And they are the last people who can put things right because they have been in denial, or it was their fault in the first place. Which is where the KPMG Business Recovery practice came in. And it was satisfying to help businesses to recover and to see the look of fear gradually leave the faces of the people in the organisation.

As soon as we were back at base the training continued. I snatched a few days here and there to spend time with Polly and with my parents.

And then I got caught up in the Labouchère case. I had just been transferred to the Forensic Services Investigations department when a whistleblower at a boutique investment bank called Labouchère Frères blew his whistle by telling the Serious Fraud Office that they might find it worthwhile to look into some transactions the bank had made with a certain Russian oligarch called Vladimir Zukhov. KPMG were seconded by the Serious Fraud Office to help to conduct an investigation.

A sharp-eyed manager at KPMG remembered from my CV that I spoke fluent Russian. I was called in to a meeting where a senior lecturer in Russian from the Open University had been retained to test whether or not my claim was true. There were no flies on KPMG. As it happened my claim was absolutely true and the OU lecturer was soon quite satisfied that I would be more than capable of understanding and translating anything spoken or written in Russian. So I was included in the KPMG team on the case.

The next thing to happen was that the whistleblower was murdered in a most bloodthirsty way and his dismembered body was dumped in a plastic bin liner in the Thames near Charing Cross Bridge where it was discovered by a dog which was being taken for an early morning walk by its owner. It was low tide and the dog just wouldn't leave the object alone so the owner had to climb down onto the shingle at the edge of the river where he found the corpse. Poor man, he was terribly affected by what he found, and had to have counselling before any sense could be got out of him and he could give the police a coherent statement.

The assassination put the investigation into a completely different context as it was now a murder case as well as fraud and this brought in the Metropolitan Police. Everyone who was working for the prosecution had to have twenty-four hour police protection. We spent nearly all our time in an office in Whitehall. All the necessary papers were brought in for us to sift through and to catalogue and analyse including hundreds of emails and bank documents and copies of transactions, many of them in Russian.

I worked nearly eighteen hours a day for three or four weeks. In the end I realised that there had been a massive money-laundering operation going on which had been further complicated by dozens of shipping documents involving a 'missing trader' fraud and a VAT carousel which turned out to have defrauded the Customs and Excise of a total of €2 billion of VAT because each time the company which owed the tax just disappeared after each trade and a new company was formed for the next transaction.

The money-laundering scheme added up to a further €6 billion. The incriminating evidence was incorporated in a series of emails in a kind of cypher Russian code which was based on a line from a poem by Boris Paternak which I recognised quite by accident. Immediately the code was cracked the whole mystery was solved and the extent of the fraud became clear.

The codebreaker working for the prosecution service was a brilliant oddball called Alexander Frenkel. He was about my age, very tall and thin with prematurely white hair and he wore dark glasses because of his weak eyesight. Thinking about it, I suppose he was an albino. We became good friends and working with him lightened the load and brought some humour to the proceedings.

Alex had an extraordinary mixture of talents and interests. For example, he knew the whole of Mozart's works by heart and had catalogued them using the Köchel numbers and interspersed his own numbering system for those works which didn't have a Köchel number. You could play him a snatch of any Mozart work and he would immediately recognise it and tell you the date it was written, its title and Köchel number as well as the name of the instrumentalist and orchestra performing the work.

Alex also had an obsession with Olympic athletics records, again he could tell you the result of any event at any Olympic Games with the names of the first three athletes in each final and their times or distances and the date of the event.

But Alex's greatest passion was chess. He was a brilliant player and a fount of knowledge on the game. He had a huge collection of books on chess, knew the names and details of every grandmaster you cared to name and with his phenomenal memory the moves of practically every important game in the history of chess.

Alex was also very well-read and had he wished he could have specialised in maths or any of the sciences which he chose but he loved games and quizes and puzzles and so he found codebreaking an easy way to make a living and to tell the truth he became rather a dilettante.

Alex was a "living database of trivia" as he self-deprecatingly put it. He was also probably the most successful codebreaker since the palmy days of Bletchley Park and by the time I first met him his reputation among his peers was world-renowned. He made short work of the rather cumbersome code being used by Zukhov.

Prosecutions for fraud are very often unsuccessful, mainly because they are always complex and also because they are usually tried by jury, and it is often impossible to persuade twelve good men - or women - and true to bring a guilty verdict, particularly because they don't grasp the financial details or understand the jargon.

So, in the Labouchère case the SFO and the Met were determined that their case should be absolutely watertight and we had to go through each and every item time after time and rehearse the prosecuting counsel in their questioning depending on different replies which might be made by the defendent. It was very exacting and tough work for everyone concerned.

Just before the trial started I gave my police 'escort' the slip to meet Polly for tea at the Ritz, a favourite haunt for us as it was a good tea in lovely surroundings and we could chat uninterrupted. After she'd poured out our tea and chosen her first sandwich she turned to me and said:

"Tom, I've been offered a terrific job at UNESCO in Paris. I'm to be part of a team to study developing economies, especially their agriculture, and it's a real challenge. They want me to create graphics to illustrate statistics for the WFO to use in highlighting food shortages and surpluses to try to anticipate potential famines and how to deal with them".

"And have you accepted it?" I asked, with a sinking feeling.

"Of course" she replied "I couldn't exactly refuse could I?" She could tell I was upset, she could always read me like a book, "anyway you're so involved with this case of yours we might not be able to meet that often – as soon as you're free you can come over to Paris and we'll spend a week-end together". And that was that.

I was rather silent during the rest of our tea and made the excuse that I had to get back to Whitehall, so we pecked each other on the cheek and parted. It was a dismal feeling. On the way home I kept wishing that I'd had the guts to ask Polly to marry me, there'd been dozens of opportunities during the past few years but I'd always shied away from it. Now she was gone, and to Paris of all places, and I was stuck in this dreadful training contract and even worse in this ghastly Labouchère case. Damn, damn, damn.

You feel very exposed sitting in the witness box at the Old Bailey. Surrounded by dozens of pairs of eyes and being questioned by bewigged learned friends who are anything but friendly is one of the most nervewracking experiences you can imagine.

On the whole the case went pretty well right from the start. The prosecution counsel were very clinical. They brought Zukhov back to the point each time he tried to stray. I gave my evidence clearly and concisely. I explained the translation of the documents from Russian to English and the relevance of the bills of lading and the other shipping documents.

As I was finishing my last piece of evidence I happened to glance at Zukhov who was sitting immobile in the dock with a small notebook in one hand and a gold ballpoint pen in the other. He looked straight at me with a sardonic smile. He was a heavily built florid man, handsome in a way with thick dark hair, but the bags under his eyes and his sagging facial muscles spoiled his looks. He held my gaze for what seemed an eternity and then he drew the tip of his gold pen slowly across his throat in a rather threatening gesture. I tried to tell myself that this was theatrical nonsense but it left me with an uneasy feeling all the same. I was mighty relieved when he was later found guilty on all counts and sent down for twenty years. And he'd be brought back to be tried for murder when the Met were ready.

A couple of days later, during the cross examination of one the Labouchère Frères executives, a Court Official came over to our table and handed me an envelope. *Telephone Message for Mr T Verity* it said on the outside. I ripped it open. "Bad news. Please call. Effie". I got permission to leave the courtroom for a few minutes and called my mother on my cellphone from a small ante room.

"Oh Tommy darling" she said "Beel is dead". I couldn't believe my ears.

"What?" I said, "how did it happen? How are you? Where are you?".

"I am at home", she replied. "Beel died in hospital. He was taken ill at work. I need you to help me". She sounded very lost and very small somehow.

"I'll come as soon as I can", I said and switched off my mobile.

I suddenly felt there was a curse on this Labouchère case. I also felt trapped and helpless.

Then I thought of my mother and how distressed she must be, my father meant everything to her, and I took a deep breath and pulled myself together. I went back into the courtroom and told my senior what had happened. He was immediately sympathetic and asked the Judge if he could have a private word with him and the defending counsel. The Judge agreed. Both counsels approached the bench. My senior spoke to the Judge in low tones. The Judge looked across at me.

"It's nearly time for lunch" he said, "and as it's Friday the Court is adjourned until ten o'clock on Monday morning", wherupon he rose and everyone in the Court stood while he swept out. I thanked my senior and bolted for the exit and hailed a cab which was going past with its light on. It was pouring with rain. In no time we arrived at Cadogan Street.

Effie greeted me with a tear-stained face. I hugged her for what seemed an age and felt her shuddering as she let go her pent-up emotions. Slowly her sobs subsided and she wiped her eyes and looked up at me. We went into the kitchen and she sat at the table while I made a cup of tea for each of us. I sat down next to her and held her hands in mine. She told me what had happened.

My father had been working long hours at his oil company, running the renewable energy department, very much involved with plans for a huge offshore wind farm off the Scottish coast. It was to be the biggest of its type in Europe when it was completed. One of the problems had been that in common with all cutting-edge technologies the parameters keep changing, and a new type of turbine blade had just been designed with an angled tip like the wing of a modern jet plane, which in theory could have improved the performance of the turbine. This had meant that Bill had decided to halt the production of several hundred turbine blades while tests were carried out on prototypes of the new blades in a wind tunnel at Southampton University.

The Board was unhappy with the delay and this had put extra pressure on Bill. He'd been working late in his office when he had suddenly collapsed. A colleague sounded the alarm and a paramedic team arrived in about ten minutes and he was rushed to Westminster Hospital. It was of no avail, Bill was dead on arrival, he had had a massive pulmonary embolism. There was nothing they could do.

"Poor Beel", said my mother "he worked so hard, he took his job so seriously, he never took any time off for a long time now. He worried about all the other people in his department, what would happen if it wasn't successful. He was often awake in the night thinking about it". She paused.

"Beel always told me he would have plenty of time for relaxing when he retired. Now it will never happen. And what shall I do without him?" She was wringing her hands in her Russian way, she looked so frail and miserable all dressed in black, my heart went out to her and I realised that for the first time in my life I would have to look after a parent, certainly for the next few days and until my father was buried.

4

My father's funeral took place at St Simon's church in Milner Street and he was buried in a plot in the nearby graveyard, next to his own parents. There was a large congregation for the service. It made me realise how popular he'd been and how many things he'd been involved with during his life, and how much I would miss him.

As well as friends and relations and people from the oil company and the City, there were cricketers, university professors, natural historians, mountaineers, and even the top brass from the Red Cross. There were several tributes from well-known men and women and the address was given by the Dean of St Paul's Cathedral who had been at Cambridge with Bill.

There was a wake at the church hall afterwards and I'd arranged for Searcies to do the catering. "We're going to miss Bill", said the Chairman of the Red Cross to me "he was one of our greatest supporters and an absolutely brilliant fundraiser". I tried not to show my surprise. He went on "whenever there was an international disaster Bill was somehow able to motivate local people to provide support. He was also a prime mover in ensuring that all the money collected for the Red Cross actually got to the people who it was meant for".

My mother's sister Olga came over from Petersburg in time for the funeral and stayed with her for a while. She was a great comfort. I visited as often as possible within the constraints of the Labouchère case which rumbled on at the Old Bailey. I tried to help Effie with little things like going through my father's personal effects but she just didn't want any help.

"Don't touch anything just for now Tommy", she said "leave it all as he left it".

I thought this was a bad idea, she was turning his room and belongings into a sort of shrine, and it would make it more and more difficult to deal with the longer it went on, but she wouldn't be persuaded. Then I was worried about what she would do all alone in the house when Olga finally left to go back to Petersburg.

At least as an executor to my father's will I would be able to deal with all the paperwork and help the lawyers to start obtaining probate and changing the bank accounts and so on.

One evening I arrived at the house in time for supper to find the two women busy packing their suitcases.

"I'm going back to Petersburg to stay with Olga", Effie announced, "she thinks it will do me good to have a change of scene. We leave tomorrow".

I felt quite relieved and I said I thought it was a very good idea. They had already booked their flight so I arranged to take them to Heathrow in time to catch their plane. Effie was very silent during the journey to the airport and said she didn't want me to wait with them. She clung to me as we said goodbye.

"As soon as this wretched case is over I'll take a week off and come over to see you in Petersburg", I said. Effie didn't look at me, she just stroked my back and then walked away. Olga made a sympathetic grimace at me and then she kissed me and hurried off to look after her sister. I watched them go through the automatic doors and I felt really miserable.

Back at the Old Bailey it was business as usual. After weeks of evidence and arguing fine legal points the judge gave his summing up. He left nothing to chance. He took the jury step by step through all the stuff they'd heard. He emphasised the seriousness of the charges. Without actually saying so he made it very clear that he expected them to bring in a verdict of guilty to all charges. The jury retired. They took days to reach a verdict.

I spent all the time available whilst waiting for the jury to make up their minds working on my studies so as to be up to speed for the internal KPMG exams which were due to be held within the next fortnight. It was essential to pass these exams before the firm would allow me to take the Institute Finals. I concentrated on absolutely every aspect of each subject, going over and over again all the previous exam papers I could get hold of. I worked during the day and through much of the night. By the time the jury came back with their verdicts I was ready for the tests.

The jury found all three of the accused guilty on all counts. The judge released the jury and all witnesses and said he would sentence the defendents the following Tuesday. We all went home with sighs of relief.

I passed the internal tests and was told I could sit the Finals when they took place in a month's time. The firm gave me written notes on all the papers we'd taken and these were helpful in deciding which areas I neded to brush up on before the public exams. So it was back to studying again with no let up.

In the event I passed the finals quite easily. This was very much thanks to KPMG's training as well as hard work on my part. I now had to decide what to do next in my career. KPMG offered me a job in any department in the firm I chose which was flattering. I asked if I could have a few weeks to decide and this they granted. For a few evenings I just chilled out and went out to dinner with various friends, including Alex Frenkel.

After one evening playing chess with Alex I got back home to hear the telephone ringing inside the flat and I hurriedly put the key in the lock to open the door and get inside before the caller could ring off. It was my aunt Olga calling from Petersburg.

"Tommy, I am so sorry but your mother Evgenia is dead". I stood inside the hall absolutely stunned.

"Are you there? Tommy, are you there? Did you hear what I said?" she asked.

"Yes, I'm here", I replied.

"Oh Tommy, it is so sad and terrible. Poor Evgenia could not forget your father. She could not sleep, she could not eat. She got thinner and thinner and had dark rings under her eyes. I took her several times to the doctor, he gave her sleeping pills. I asked her why not call you Tommy to ask you to come to Petersburg to spend a little time with her. She wouldn't do it. Then she took a whole bottle of sleeping pills and this morning she did not wake up. Oh, Tommy I am so sorry to tell you this........." and she began to sob.

"You mustn't blame yourself", I said. "I should have come to Petersburg to look after her myself".

"When can you come?" asked Olga. "We must wait for you to be here. Then we can decide what to do about the funeral".

"I'll get the first plane I can", I said "I'll let you know as soon as I've booked and made arrangements. Thank you Olga, this is very hard for you. Thank you", and I hung up.

Strangely, the only thing I could think of as I stood in the dark hallway was Lady Bracknell's words to Jack Worthing.

"To lose one parent, Mr Worthing, may be regarded as a misfortune; to lose both looks like carelessness".

It wasn't funny though.

5

My mother's funeral took place in a Russian Orthodox church near Olga's home, and Effie was buried in a tiny churchyard next to the church.

"It is good that Evgenia is buried here", said Olga later, "it means that you will have to come visit me often. I am your special friend and relation now". She stroked my hand.

All the Russian relatives were more than kind and tried to cheer me up. We got very drunk on very expensive vodka the last night before I flew back to England and I felt lousy on the plane coming home. One of the air hostesses kept glancing at me very disapprovingly for the whole flight, I think she was quite sure I was going to throw up all over the plane. I managed to keep everything down all right and got a taxi home from Heathrow, I didn't trust myself on public transport.

I paid off the cabby and let myself into my parents' home in Cadogan Street. It was my home now but I felt no pleasure in its ownership as I went inside, just sadness and remorse. I went round the house opening the windows and the shutters to let in the air and light. Then I went up to my old bedroom and fell on to the bed fully dressed. I slept for ten hours.

Next morning I showered and shaved and went out to a local café for breakfast. I sat disconsolate over my black coffee. Polly had gone to Paris, my father and mother were dead. What a mess. I looked around the café at the other people eating breakfast. They were just ordinary folk starting another ordinary day. I recognised some of them as neighbours who lived either in Cadogan Street or just around the corner. I asked the waitress for some more coffee.

"Off to work, are you?", she asked conversationally.

It was an epiphany moment. I looked at the waitress, paused, and then "Yes actually I am", I replied.

Despite everything I still had my job with KPMG. I suddenly knew what I would do. I would finish my training contract and elect to work in the Business Recovery department and learn as much as I could. As soon as I was able to do so I would get a practising certificate and start my own business. I would concentrate on working for small clients who needed the very best advice and try to build up a local practice somewhere.

I went home and changed and took the tube from Sloane Square to Mansion House and walked to the

KPMG Building. Everyone seemed pleased to see me. Everyone was very sympathetic about my bereavements. My senior welcomed the fact that I wanted to join the Business Recovery group. In the meantime, he said, I should take time off to sort things out at home and take a short holiday and then start fresh at the beginning of September. He shook my hand.

"You got first prize in your exams", he said "you probably hadn't heard?"

"No, I hadn't" I replied, quite amazed.

"The senior partner has been trumpeting it around all over the place", he said "almost as if he won the thing himself!", then he smiled and shook my hand again.

"See you on first September" he said.

"Thanks", I replied and then I walked to the lift.

6

The first thing I needed to do was deal with my parents' wills. Fortunately my father's old friend Freddy Garland-Wells was also his solicitor and he was very matter-of-fact about everything and quite supportive.

"You can leave everything to me to deal with if you wish", he said. "Your parents' affairs are very tidy. There are a few pecuniary legacies, otherwise they left everything to you. After a minimal amount of Inheritance Tax you will have a tidy sum in cash and investments, and the house of course. I'll prepare all the papers for Probate. In the meantime you have enough money to live on, I suppose?"

"Yes thanks" I replied "and thank you for your help".

"Delighted, my boy, your father was a very valued old friend. It's a sad day for all of us", and he saw me to the door.

I went out to Ealing on the tube and visited our old allotment. Mrs Grodzinski was still there, friendly and rock solid. She was sad when I told her about my mother. I told her that I wouldn't be able to carry on with the allotment and that maybe she knew of someone who would like to take it on. She said her son Wilf would be pleased to have it, his wife had just had twins and it would help to be able to grow more food for the family.

I took the train to Cambridge and stayed a week-end with my aunt Georgina and Simon and we chatted about my father's family and she told me about his childhood. Georgina was especially sad about Effie, she had really liked her from the first time she'd gone to stay.

Georgina and Simon told me what their sons Tristram and Toby were up to now. I remembered the holidays I'd spent with the family when I was a boy and what a good time I'd had on the Norfolk Broads with my two cousins. Now Tristram was a chemical engineer with a phamaceutical company and Toby had just qualified as a Chartered Accountant with PwC.

When I left to return to London Georgina said:

"There's always a room here for you if you need one", then she kissed me on the cheek and turned away, she couldn't hide her emotions any more.

Back in London my next task was to reply to all the letters and messages of condolence and kind thoughts received. I also had to inform all the usual people like the utilities and the local council and the dentist and several stores and anyone else of my mother's death.

Then I had to go through all my parents' belongings and decide what to do with everything. As my mother hadn't been able to face dealing with my father's things I had to do both parents' stuff. Once I'd gritted my teeth and made a start it was quite therapeutic. I disposed of all the personal bits and pieces in large black plastic bags and put them into the garbage bin, things like toothpaste, razors, shaving cream, my mother's toiletries, underwear and so on.

Then I looked through all the other clothes and shoes. A few items of my father's fitted me and I kept the nicest. I went into the Oxfam shop in King's Road and the manageress agreed to come to the house in a few days' time and help me sort anything which would be useful to Oxfam. After she'd left there were very few things to dispose of, the rest was furniture, pictures and books, and family memorabilia.

I hadn't realised what a hoarder my father had been. He had the most eclectic collection of things I had ever seen. Cigarette cards (of cricketers of course), lead toy soldiers, things from his career in the oil industry including a fabulous series of very old photographs of early wildcat drillers in the US and some sepia photographs taken in Persia in the early days of BP.

There was a numbered collection of birds' eggs in the drawers of a purpose-built cabinet with a notebook which had precise details of where each egg had been found with the date, location and in some cases sketches of the actual nest and its site.

There were masses of books and some beautiful small statuettes, also groups of sihouettes of members of the Verity family going back four generations. Then I discovered a family tree in a leather-bound ledger with a page for each small family group and links to other groups of the same generation or of parents or children. All annotated with details of each person's life.

I came across a bundle of my parents' love letters, which after some hesitation I read through. They were very touching and affectionate and made me weep. I also had to laugh at some of Effie's English in several of her notes to 'dear Beel'.

Effie's own belongings included a collection of hand-made dolls representing every part she had danced with the Kirov, lovingly dressed in miniature copies of the actual costumes she had worn for each part. There were dozens of playbills of all the ballets she had performed in, all carefully preserved.

All these things were reminders of a bygone age and I determined to keep them carefully preserved for my children if I were lucky enough to have any.

I cleaned the house from top to bottom and tidied everything up and made the beds ready for any visitors. I moved my belongings out of my flat and into the main bedroom in the house in Cadogan Street and I put my flat with an agent with instructions to let it.

Then on the spur of the moment I decided on a walking holiday in the Italian Dolomites and I took the train from Victoria with several changes, ending with a two hour bus ride to Cortina d'Ampezza - the railway had been closed for a long time - with my rucksack and waterproofs and a sleeping bag and a Baedeker Guide and a copy of *A Time of Gifts* by Patrick Leigh Fermor to read on the train, wearing my walking boots for the whole journey.

I stayed a night in Cortina at the old Railway Hotel where we arrived very late in the evening and I set off the next morning after breakfast, with a packed lunch. It was a superb day, the sky was a very pale blue and it was warm and sunny and on the lower slopes there were late summer flowers and a few berries forming on the trees. As I got higher I drank in the views across the valleys above the conifer forests to the peaks in the far distance. Eventually I stopped for lunch, sitting on a large boulder. There were some clouds coming up behind the ranges to the east but I didn't think they would come to much so I decided to press on a bit.

Quite suddenly I found myself in thick cloud and it became very cold and rather threatening. I got out the Baedeker and saw that there was a mountain rescue hut about two kilometers further down the track from where I was, so I made for it as fast as I could. It actually took me nearly an hour to reach the hut.

The storm overtook me very quickly. The conditions were so bad that I couldn't see more than a few centimeters in front of me. Also, it had become so cold and icy that every step was an ordeal and my eyebrows were covered in frost. I cursed myself for not taking more care over checking out the weather and letting the hotel know where I was planning to walk to. My father had always stressed the rules which applied to being in the mountains and I had failed to obey them this time.

At last I saw the hut in front of me. There were no lights at the window and no smoke was coming from the chimney, so nobody could be there. I hoped that there would be a supply of wood for the stove and some tea bags or tinned soup. I struggled with the door in the wind and entered the hut, the door slammed shut behind me. The storm howled outside. I located the paraffin lamp and lit it, and stood taking in the surroundings and the contents of the interior. At least I was safe until the storm blew over. A woman's voice suddenly spoke, making me jump out of my skin. It was a familiar voice and it said "Look what the cat brought in!". It was Polly.

She was shivering so badly that her teeth were literally chattering. I had often read about this in books and rather dismissed the phrase, but now here was Polly and her teeth were really making an irregular involuntary noise as they chattered together. Her face was almost blue with cold and her hair was wet and matted. Her clothes were soaked through.

I quickly built a heap of kindling wood and logs in the stove and lit the fire. Then I filled the water jug and put it on top of the stove to boil. Then I turned to Polly.

"Where are your dry clothes and your pack?" I asked.

"Lost" she gasped "all lost", and she looked as if she was going to cry.

"We've got to get you out of these wet clothes", I said and I undid her zips and buttons and poppers and velcro and peeled her clothes off her. Then I got my towel out of my pack and rubbed her dry. Next I got out my sleeping bag and helped her into it, and sat her on some cushions in front of the stove which was by now a roaring fire. I made us each a mug of scalding hot tea and found some biscuits in a tin. Then I rubbed her back and tried to bring some life and feeling back into her bones. Slowly she recovered.

I wrung out all her clothes and hung them to dry on a line in front of the fire. Then I sat next to her and put my arm around her. She promptly fell asleep with her head on my shoulder. Later, I too fell asleep after I'd stoked up the fire and when I awoke I saw Polly looking intently into my face. She grinned.

"Hadn't you better get into your sleeping bag?" she enquired.

"No, you keep it for now", I answered.

"I meant get into it with me, stupid", she said. I gazed at her for a long time. All the old feelings came rushing back. My God, how I had missed her. I stood up and took off all my clothes and slipped into the sleeping bag alongside Polly, facing her so that I could feel the whole length of her pressed into me. There wasn't much room for us both.

"Now you can warm me up", she said. So I did.

7

We had a great deal to say to bring each other up to date. When I asked her how she had come to be in the hut, Polly told me she had suggested a walking holiday in the Dolomites with colleagues from UNESCO. She remembered how beautiful it was from the time we had walked there when we'd been at Imperial College, and she had persuaded the others to give it a try.

André, one of the Frenchmen in the party, thought he was entitled to seduce any woman he chose and his fancy lighted on Polly. She wasn't having any of it and this made him extremely unpleasant towards her. From then on the trek became a bore.

Then, the previous afternoon the storm suddenly broke and Polly, who'd been lagging behind the others to avoid contact with André had suddenly found herself detached from the group. She rushed forward to catch up, tripped and fell and lost her grip on her pack which slid along the path and then plunged into a gorge. Luckily she had struggled on along the track and come across the hut, where I had found her. I dreaded to

47

think what might have happened if I hadn't come along, but of course I didn't say so.

"Good old Sir Galahad" said Polly, but inside her mocking exterior I sensed a really warm and appreciative feeling. Suddenly she grasped me to her.

"Let's live together from now on", she said "we've been apart for far too long. I don't really want to live without you".

"Is this a proposal of marriage?" I asked, catching her mood.

"If that's what you want, yes", she answered.

"Then I accept", I said, and it sealed my fate for ever.

When I told Polly that both my parents had died she was visibly upset.

"They were such lovely people", she said "both of them so warm and interesting and so very different. I can't believe I'll never see them again", she paused, then "darling, you must miss them terribly", and she hugged me tight for a long time. It was the first time Polly had ever called me darling.

The dawn broke fine and bright and it felt good to be together in the hut, just the two of us alone. Our clothes were warm and dry by now and we both dressed and had mugs of tea and the rest of the biscuits for breakfast, sitting outside the hut looking across at the magnificent panorama, the fresh snow on the peaks and upper slopes of Rocca Pictore shone pink in the sun.

We tidied the hut, left some money in the tin and closed up all the windows and shutters and the door and started walking slowly back down the path towards Cortina, chatting intimately and comfortably together.

It became warm as well as bright and we were strolling along in our shirt sleeves when round a bend in the track we saw a group of people hurrying up towards us.

"It's UNESCO", said Polly "that's the end of our peace for a while".

"Where were you?" asked a tall woman as they reached us and this was a signal for a barrage of questions in different languages. When the babble ceased, Polly said:

"This is my fiancée Tom Verity. We arranged to meet in the Mountain Rescue Hut last night. Why, what's wrong?".

They all looked rather stumped. Polly introduced each of them to me. We started walking back towards Cortina again, Polly holding my hand. They were not completely convinced but clearly didn't want to make fools of themselves so they kept quiet.

Eventually we reached the Railway Hotel. Polly said she would go and collect her bags from the hostel where they were staying and come back and move in with me for the two days which were left for their trip. When she returned she was finding it hard not to laugh.

"Their faces were a study, weren't they?" she said. "they're a pretty hard-boiled bunch but this time they were quite bemused. I told them I was leaving UNESCO and taking up a position in London immediately. I'll fly back to Paris with them just to collect my things and come straight over to London and join you".

"What position are you taking up?" I asked, rather mystified.

"We could work our way through the Kama Sutra if you like", she replied.

I laughed. "You really are outrageous", I said "but thank God for it".

8

When Polly moved into Cadogan Street with me she changed the whole atmosphere of the house. After my parents had died the place had seemed rather like a mausoleum, dingy and sad. Polly added her own style, so that everything seemed lighter and brighter. She put window boxes on every window sill and there were dozens of plants in all sorts of different types of tubs and pots in the back yard, including vegetables, salads and fruits. She rearranged the living room so that it bacame more feminine and airy. She sang a lot too, mostly tunes from shows she'd been to, and she had a sweet voice which lifted my spirits.

I went back to work in the Business Recovery unit at KPMG at the beginning of September. Our first client was a household name in the carpet industry whose financial controls had got completely out of control. The business was based in London, so there wasn't much travelling to start with.

Polly did some free-lance work for Oxfam helping the fundraisers to redesign their graphics so as to provide clearer information and persuade people to donate to the charity. We quickly settled into a routine of doing our jobs during the day and enjoying the evenings and week-ends together.

One bonus was that I got to know Polly's family much better. I had only ever met them before at university functions when they came to support Polly and to celebrate her successes with her. Now we spent more time with them and I grew to like and admire her parents. Their lives in Romania under the Ceaucescu regime had been pretty tough and it had become almost impossible for her father to do his work as a doctor in a children's hospital. Eventually he got a post working in the London Hospital in Whitechapel.

Adelbert Kovacs became one of the leading specialists in Britain in child leukaemia. Polly's mother Camelia was a qualified midwife and together they were a formidable team.

Polly had two younger brothers, Stefan and Angelo, tall and athletic like their father. Polly looked more like her mother who definitely had Romany blood. The whole family was welcoming and hospitable and very sympathetic to me when they found out that both my parents had died so suddenly. As Polly's fiancée I was immediately accepted into the family without any reservation and I felt I belonged again.

However, Camelia made it very clear that she was unhappy that Polly and I were living together unmarried. Polly said we would get married if it was just a quiet family affair. There was no chance of that, Camelia wanted a proper family wedding for her only daughter, so Polly gave way in the end.

We were married in the Church of St George in the East in Whitechapel, with the reception afterwards in the church hall. There were crowds of people and it was a truly international affair and I must say that Polly and I enjoyed it very much.

We went away on our honeymoon to Northumberland and we toured around and visited the Farne Islands and several castles and National Trust properties including Cragside which I found fascinating.

Back home we planned our future together. We decided we wanted to live in the countryside, and we hit on the idea that we would try and find a smallholding close to a country town in which I could set up my own accountancy practice and Polly could work as a free-lance statistician. As soon as my training contract was completed I could apply for a practicing certificate, and this is what happened.

We sold our Cadogan Street house and with most of the proceeds we bought an old converted barn with ten acres and some outbuildings, situated a couple of miles outside Horsham in Sussex. It was called Sedgwick Farm.

I rented a small office in the town, opposite Sainsbury's car park so that clients could park free for up to a couple of hours within a minute's walk of my office. The office was on the ground floor of what had once been a rather charming old cottage in a row of small homes.

There was a fireplace in the main room which had been bricked-up but the mantelpiece was still there. I spent a couple of days painting the two rooms and the kitchen and the lavatory with a job lot of Apricot White emulsion paint, laid some new carpet, hung a few pictures on the walls, put all my technical books on the shelves, and screwed my name plate to the outside wall next to the front door.

I also put an advertisement in the local newspaper. And the phone never stopped ringing.

Here's what the ad said

THOMAS VERITY : ACCOUNTS AND TAX SERVICE

SPEEDY AND AFFORDABLE

NO BUSINESS TOO SMALL

PLEASE CALL 0845 124 458 FOR A FREE CONSULTATION

BEST COFFEE IN TOWN

I made several resolutions when I started: never to wear a suit or a tie, always to tell clients the truth and not necessarily what they wanted to hear, to agree fixed fees with clients before I started a piece of work so as not to have to waste time logging the hours spent, and always to try to do things on time. And to take at least six weeks holiday a year.

Chapter 3

1

On the first Monday morning I got to the office early to open for business. The phone rang at eight o'clock.

"Is that Thomas Verity?" said a male voice.

"Yes it is", I replied.

"My name's Frank Waller. Are you the Thomas Verity who sorted out the Labouchère case?"

"That's me" I said. The case had been widely reported in the press.

"Can I come and see you this morning?"

"Name the time" I said.

"Ten o'clock" said Frank. And so it was.

Frank arrived promptly at ten. I made us a cafetière of fresh Colombian Freetrade coffee and sat down opposite Frank at the table. He was a powerful man in his mid to late twenties with a mane of untidy thick brown hair, a clean-shaven face, blue eyes and an engaging smile. He looked straight at me.

"How can I help you?" I asked.

"My accountant was killed in a car crash" he said, "so I need someone to look after all my stuff for me. My sister and brother need a new accountant for their business too. Tim looked after their affairs as well as mine. I've come to check you out".

I realised that he was referring to Tim Berrington. I'd read about the accident in the local paper. It had been a horrendous head-on crash at two o'clock in the morning. Tim had been on his way home from visiting a client in Wolverhampton and he must have just fallen asleep as he neared his home and went straight into an oncoming lorry. Tim was much liked by everyone who knew him and he was a very good sportsman. I had never met him. There was nothing to say.

I opened my Moleskine notebook. For as long as I can remember I've kept all my notes in a succession of these legendary notebooks, writing the notes on the right-hand page and putting updates, comments or corrections on the opposite left hand page. When a notebook is full I stick a label on the front with the number of the notebook and the dates it covers and store it with the others in a fire-proof safe. The current book is the forty-second.

"Tell me your story" I said, and so he did.

2

Frank Waller had been born the eldest son of a family of six children. His parents were farmers, not exactly poor but pretty hard up, so that every penny counted and the kids were taught from an early age not to waste anything and to make do and mend and never to chuck anything away. They all had to help on the farm. They started by collecting the free-range eggs and feeding the chickens and lambs and calves and pigs, then as they got older they helped with the milking and lambing and shearing and eventually with making silage and hay.

From the beginning Frank had been handy at making and fixing things on the farm. He was very good with machinery and he could drive any kind of vehicle as soon as his feet could reach the pedals. He was musical and made his own instruments, first a guitar and later a violin.

One of their uncles had a small yacht and took the family sailing. Frank enjoyed the experience so much that he immediately set-to and built a Mirror dinghy so that the family could all go sailing on Chichester Harbour whenever they had the time. Frank never took to team sports but he loved sailing and horse riding and later skiing when he was able to afford it. The only sport he excelled in at school was judo, he was very fast and strong.

Frank had an entrepreneurial streak and when he was twelve years old he started to make money by repairing old radios which had been thrown out by people who thought they were no longer serviceable, when very often all they needed was a slight adjustment or a loose wire soldered or some simple problem fixed, and he then sold these radios.

Sometimes people asked him to repair their radios, so he charged them for doing so. After a while he did the same with television sets and later with computers.

Frank converted an old stable into a workshop and he built up a large stock of spare parts which he canibalised from radios, television sets and computers which were past redemption. He made friends with the people working at the local tip and they saved him any radios or TVs or PCs in exchange for beer money. He devised an ingenious computerised recording system for his stocks so that he could put his hands on any part within a few seconds. He started selling parts on the internet by mail-order and this made him a small fortune by the time he left sixth form college.

Whilst at college Frank had studied general science including botany and chemistry, and he had spent time working for a local nursery garden which had a tissue culture laboratory, so that by the time he took his A level exams and left college he was proficient at propagating plants from rooted cuttings and from 'plugs' grown in test tubes by micropropagation.

Frank decided not to go to university. Instead he spent some of his small fortune travelling round the world and set off on his own with nothing but a backpack. He left his sister Elinor in charge of his parts business and told her she could keep any profits she made from it whilst he was away. After going through Africa from north to south, he went to India and Sri Lanka and then on to south-east Asia.

He spent nearly six months in Australia and New Zealand travelling with a girl he'd met up with in Broome. She was having trouble with a bloke who kept trying to pester her and Frank had to sort him out. He bought a second-hand Land Rover from a cocky farmer and he and Catherine travelled on through the Kimberleys and then right across the red centre of Australia mostly on dirt roads, sleeping in a tent and cooking their food on a barbecue and making their tea in a billy.

They sailed from Sydney across the Tasman in an ocean racer which was being delivered to a member of the Auckland Yacht Club, getting a free passage in exchange for helping to sail the boat.

In New Zealand they bought a couple of bicycles and continued their nomadic lifestyle and saw almost the whole of both the North and South Islands. They cycled among large dairy herds and thousands of sheep on the green pastureland, they walked in the rain forest and they skiied in the Alps, fished in the rivers, worked for a few weeks in a vinyard, and skinny dipped in the ice-cold lakes. By the time they reached Christchurch they had fallen well and truly in love. But Kate had to get back to the North Shore Hospital to start her training as a physiotherapist so they flew from Christchurch to Sydney where they parted sadly.

Frank sold the Land Rover and bought a laptop computer and sailed in a bulk carrier carrying iron ore from Port Kembla to Japan, travelling steerage. During his time in New Zealand he had pretty well made up his mind what he was going to do when he got back to England.

The family farm was too small to support more than one family, but Frank's heart was in the countryside and he had always loved trees. In a second-hand bookshop in Christchurch he'd picked up a copy of *The Green Belt Movement* by the Nobel peace prize winner Wangari Maathai who'd been responsible for the planting of forty million trees in Africa, and this had inspired him and got him thinking.

Now that he had seen the many varieties of eucalypts and other natives in Australia and the kauri, pohutukawa, and other magnificent trees in New Zealand he thought he would try his hand at starting and running an English native tree nursery when he got back home, so he spent his time on board the ship expanding his knowledge about trees and horticulture - botany, propagation, genetics, plant pathology and brushing up on the theory of tissue culture - using his laptop as a source of information from the web. He came to the conclusion that the best way to start was to grow trees in containers, he wouldn't need much land for this and the business would be readily transportable.

He spent a couple of weeks on a whistle-stop tour of Japan and flew on to Los Angeles where he bought a Greyhound bus pass to get across the States. He was amazed at the variety of everything in America and surprised at the huge difference between rich and poor. He stopped off at several container nurseries and what he saw confirmed him in his decision. Some of the enterprises were huge which meant that he could build up a sizeable business in this way. He spent a week in New York drinking in the sights and visiting as many museums and art galleries as possible before flying back to London.

On the plane his thoughts kept returning to Kate. He had never expected to feel like this about anyone. It wasn't just the physical attraction and the touch and smell of her which made him feel this way, they had become very close friends and he'd felt able to tell her absolutely anything about himself without reservation, besides she had the most amazing sense of humour and they had several times collapsed with laughter. She was very special.

When he got home Frank told his parents and siblings what he hoped to do. They were very supportive and offered to let him have the old disused pig unit with its yard and buildings to get started and to see if he could make a go of his idea. When his nursery business began to make a profit he would be able to look for his own place to expand it.

Quite soon afterwards he got a text message: *Please call me urgently. Kate*

Frank calculated that it was half past two in the morning in Sydney, but the word 'urgently' made up his mind for him so he called the number stored on his cellphone and she answered almost immediately.

"Kate, how are you?"

"Oh Frank", she said "I'm pregnant. What should I do?"

Frank didn't hesitate. He felt breathless and elated and sick all at the same time.

"Come over to the UK as soon as you can and marry me. I can't tell you how much I've missed you".

"I've missed you too...." her voice waivered for a second or two "....oh Frank I hoped you'd react this way. But what'll we do?"

"We'll work all that out when you're here. Let me know your flight details and I'll pay for your ticket with my credit card".

"Oh thank God", was all she said, and burst into tears.

3

When Frank told the family about Kate over supper that night they were very intrigued and wanted to know all about her. It seemed perfectly natural to them that Frank had found a soulmate and they couldn't wait to meet her. But Frank was secretly worried about the future. Now suddenly he was going to have a wife and child to provide for. He had no house and his tree nursery business idea was just that, an idea. He told his sister Ellie his concerns.

"Don't forget you've still got your parts business" she said. "We haven't had time to tell you all about it yet". After supper Ellie took Frank outside to the shed where the business was housed. Their younger brother Jake went with them.

"Jake's been helping me with the business", said Ellie, "in fact he's really responsible for the expansion of it". She tapped in the code on the lock of the door, pushed it open, turned on the light and stepped aside to let Frank go in first. He stood in the doorway amazed.

Instead of the small area of the shed which had contained the parts business he had left behind there was now a space four times the size because there was an opening through the wall of the shed into the barn next door. There were racks from floor to ceiling filled with different items. In the first shed they were electronic components just as he'd left things, but in the barn there were engineered parts. On closer inspection Frank saw that these were parts from mopeds and scooters.

"Jake wanted to get a 49cc scooter when he was sixteen", said Ellie, "but they were too expensive. So he went to the scrap yard at Broadbridge Heath and found several wrecked scooters of the same make which he bought for a few quid and Dad went with him and brought them back on the trailer."

"Then I took them all apart", said Jake, "and quite easily made a complete scooter out of the best parts. I sprayed it up and got it MOT'd and licensed, and bingo I had wheels".

"Then what happened?" asked Frank.

"Well, my friends all wanted a scooter then", said Jake "so I did the same thing again and quite soon I'd built half a dozen scooters. It's amazing how many scooters get chucked away by people who haven't a clue how to fix them. They just write them off. Of course I discovered that I soon had masses of spare parts so Ellie and I decided to do the same as you'd done with the radios and TV sets and we started a mail-order business selling scooter parts. Then we expanded into motor bikes."

"All the time I was running the electronic side of your business", said Ellie, "and it just grew and grew. Every time a new model comes out people just get rid of their old stuff. The retailers aren't interested in taking anything back so we've become their undertakers so to speak. Sometimes we even get paid for taking old stock off their hands. We also pick up items from the op shops and from car boot sales. There's a sort of sub-culture of people below the throw-away society who actually want to build their own TVs and computers and radios - and scooters and bikes of course – and they need parts so we're now the first port of call for these people".

"There's a massive opportunity for repairing and recycling other mechanical stuff too", said Jake, "Ellie and I reckon that we could expand into sewing machines, pushbikes, lawn mowers, rotavators and outboard engines. We've got an arrangement with the mechanical engineering departments at Crawley College and at Chichester College. They send us students on day-release and we train them to rebuild and test machinery and equipment. They soon become very useful. One of the perks for the students is that they end up with a scooter or a motor bike at the end of the course so there's never any shortage of volunteers".

Frank was speechless. He stared around him full of surprise and pride in what his sister and brother had achieved.

"We've kept detailed records for each part of the business", said Ellie. She took down a thick notebook from a shelf on which were stacked a whole lot of manuals and handbooks.

"The electronic business made more than sixty thousand pounds last year and has nearly a hundred thousand in the bank", she continued, "and the stock's worth about the same. There'll be some tax to pay. I took out enough to pay for my own college fees and rent and expenses".

"The scooter side has forty thousand in the bank and about three times that in stock", said Jake.

"I can't take anything from you", said Frank. "You've created this business in the time I've been away. It belongs to you now".

"We've thought of that", they said in unison. Then they laughed and Jake said "You tell him".

"Well we realise you don't want to carry on with this business", said Ellie, "but we'd like to." So we thought the fairest thing would be for us to buy it off you. Then we can keep everything from now on and you can start your tree-growing business".

Frank frowned and opened his mouth to protest but Jake cut him short.

"We reckon a hundred thousand would be fair, in cash now. In five years time Ellie and I will both be millionaires, thanks to your idea".

"And that's final", said Ellie "so shut up and let's have a cup of tea to celebrate".

And that's just what they did.

4

When Kate arrived from Sydney she and Frank started to look for a home. Frank had decided not to buy a house to start with but to use his new-found capital to invest in his tree nursery project and to live on while he built the business up. They found a cottage with a garden and a stable block to rent unfurnished in a nearby village. The cottage was 'in need of restoration' as the estate agent's blurb said, but as a result the rent was low, so as soon as they'd signed the lease they set to and working together they re-equipped and redecorated the cottage from top to bottom and soon had everything ready to move in.

Frank and Kate got married in the local church as soon as Kate had got over her period of morning sickness but before she was too heavily pregnant. Her parents flew over from Sydney for the wedding and they had a small family party afterwards. Kate's parents went on to enjoy a trip around the UK and Europe and Frank and Kate decided that as they'd already had their honeymoon on their travels in Australia and New Zealand they would stay at home.

By now Frank had decided to concentrate on growing rooted cuttings of trees and to set up a micropropagation unit. Plants which are grown from cuttings or by tissue culture are clones of their parent and because they have the same genes as the lone parent from which they're made they are all identical.

The great advantage of tissue culture is that it's quite possible to grow literally thousands of plants from minute pieces taken from one plant and grown in a test tube, produced in sterile conditions and fed on a balanced diet of chemicals. Each piece can produce incredible numbers of tiny replicas of its single parent. This means that it is unnecessary to have lots of stock plants for material for cuttings, in fact a single piece taken from one plant can be enough to grow many thousands of plants.

Frank knew from the time when he worked in the local nursery that his laboratory would need three separate but connected areas for his tissue culture operation to be successful, a preparation area, a transfer room and a culture growing room. He also knew how vital it was that the lab should be absolutely clean and free of dust or any other contamination, so he knocked down one of the walls between two of the stables and lined the area top and bottom with plastic-coated board. Then he divided the space into three sections and set up shelving and cupboards and a sink in the preparation room.

Instead of buying new equipment which would have cost a fortune, Frank equipped the lab with second-hand or alternative equipment. Frank used his mother's old pressure cooker as an autoclave for sterilising everything. He made an isolation chamber out of an old box with a sheet of glass as the floor of the cabinet and fitted a single fluorescent bulb fixture for lighting and a UV germicidal lamp for sterilisation. Instead of a binocular dissecting microscope he bought a headband binocular magnifier with five times magnification.

Instead of buying culture vessels he collected thousands of baby food jars and their lids, and many more ingenious money-saving items to stock and equip his lab, at a total cost of just a few hundred pounds instead of the tens thousands of pounds it would have cost if he'd bought everything new from catalogues.

To kick-start the business Frank decided to try and get a contract to grow plugs and rooted cuttings for other nurserymen to grow on. This would provide a regular income while he experimented with his tree-growing plan. It would also allow him to find out what he was best at. He wrote personal letters to the owners and managers of all the local nurseries which he could find in the Growers Annual Handbook, offering to quote for growing plants for them.

Out of the blue Frank received an enquiry to grow some orchids for Robinsons, a nursery based in Hampshire which had a chain of about twenty garden centres. Robinsons' orchid supplier, Phillips Propagators, which had grown all Robinsons' orchids up till then, had been taken over by a multi-national and had switched all its production to Malasia.

Robinsons' directors had decided to continue to source their orchids in the UK, from a local grower if possible and they decided to ask Frank to become their supplier. It was a gamble for Robinsons and a huge opportunity for Frank. Robinsons would provide Frank with all the original plant material for propagating the orchids as long as Frank committed his production a hundred percent to Robinsons until he could satisfy their demand. Frank put his tree-growing idea on hold and concentrated on learning as much as possible about orchids as fast as he could.

In the event Frank grew tens of thousands of orchids for Robinsons and by the end of the second year the business had expanded so rapidly and so enormously that he had been able to move the whole enterprise to a site on the Chichester Plain which had about ten acres of glasshouses which had been built by a Dutch tomato grower but which had been abandoned a couple of years ago when the company went into administration.

5

Frank broke off his story and stared at me. I stopped writing my notes and looked back at him. We had finished three cafetieres of coffee and a bottle of water but my mouth was still dry. It had seemed a long and intense two hour interview. There was a protracted silence. My hand ached from all the writing.

"Will you take us on?" asked Frank, "we badly need some good advice".

"Yes, of course" I replied.

"When can you come and look around?"

"How about Friday morning" I said.

"Fine", said Frank "I'll see you then. I'll send you details of how to find us in an email."

I saw him to the door and watched him cross the road and walk towards the car park, then I went back into the office and cleared away the coffee things. I sat thinking about his story, thumbing through my notebook and adding a few notes. The phone rang and interrupted my train of thought. It was Polly.

"How's it going?" she asked.

"Good", I said "I just got two new clients and heard a rather interesting story".

"I'm in town", said Polly "can you meet me in ten minutes at Waterstones coffee shop and have a snack lunch?".

"I'll be there", I said.

Just as I was leaving the office a courier delivered a small packet. I signed for it and went back inside and put it on my desk. On the label it said the sender was my father's old oil company. I decided to wait to open it when I got back from lunch, and hurried off to meet Polly.

The Santa Fé coffee shop was on the first floor in Waterstones' book shop. As well as excellent coffee it also provided very good snack lunches including a variety of bagels. When I arrived I found Polly sitting at a table for two by the window.

"I ordered you your usual", she said.

We're all creatures of habit I guess, and I'm no exception. I always have a *Scottish* bagel which is a poppy seed bagel filled with cream cheese and smoked salmon. I always mean to try a different variety but every time I weaken and go back to the good old

Scottish. It arrived with Polly's *Roma* and two mugs of caffé latté almost as soon as I sat down.

"Guess what", said Polly "I've been offered a most interesting job. I got an email out of the blue from my old supervisor at the Office for National Statistics. He's now working for the biggest publisher of educational books in the country and he'd just heard that I left UNESCO so he wrote and asked me if I'd like to write a series of illustrated articles for schools and colleges on a history of diagrams. I've got carte blanche to do it in my own way and he'll even pay me for providing him with a scheme and a layout for the first twelve articles. What do you think?"

"Good for you", I said "it sounds right up your street" then after a pause, in my typically cautious way "we've got a hell of a lot to do what with this new assignment of yours, and building the practice up, and getting Sedgwick Farm in order!"

"Better to wear out than rust out" retorted Polly.

6

When I got back to the office I opened up the packet from BP. Inside there were a couple of small photographs in frames, one was of my mother dressed fo her part as Lise in La Fille Mal Gardée which she had danced at the Kirov, the other was of the three of us in the Lake District taken on a family holiday. There was an old notebook with a red tooled hard cover. Attached to the notebook was an envelope with my name on it. Inside was a rather charming letter from the Company Secretary of BP telling me that these were the only personal effects which they had found in my father's office and hoping that I was keeping well.

I placed the photographs on the mantelpiece and sat down at my desk and opened the notebook. There were pages and pages of my father's neat handwriting, all in fountain pen, with headings underlined and the date when each entry had been written. It was a sort of commonplace book. I read it through at one sitting.

There were poems, by T S Elliot, Robert Frost, W B Yeats and a particularly memorable one by A S J Tessimond called *Day Dream*. There were well-known sayings and lesser-known sayings, including some by Oscar Wilde and some by Mark Twain. There were notes on books my father had read and films he'd seen and plays he'd been to, especially plays by Chekhov. All just commonplace stuff.

Then about a year ago the entries had changed in content and had ceased to be reflections and experiences of other people's work and become his own personal thoughts and concerns.

The gist of his writings was that he was becoming increasingly concerned about the sustainability of the world's resources. He alluded to Fritz Schumacher's seminal work *Small is Beautiful* which expounds this very idea, that the world's resources are running out and that we are living off capital.

Even worse, we are wrecking our environment by a mad dash for growth, cutting down the rain forest, continuously spraying noxious chemicals on crops to prevent weeds or pests from invading them (here he referred to Rachel Carson's *Silent Spring*) or building whole towns on good agricultural land which should be used to feed the increasing population of the planet, and overfishing the oceans so that in a few years time wild fish will be but a memory.

Water is already a serious problem, he wrote, and soon will become scarcer and possibly more valuable than oil. Food will also become scarce and much more expensive and this could result in mass starvation. The lights will go out because of our reliance on fossil fuels which will eventually run out. It was a litany of disaster.

But there were solutions. There were things that each of us could do as individuals, things that businesses and scientists could do, and things that governments could do. The problem was persuading people to take the necessary action. This required political will and education.

My father had then started to elaborate on his solutions. His last enty in the notebook which was dated the day before he had died was a reference to a series of mandalas which he had drawn and hidden safely at home. These mandalas would form the basis of all the necessary action to prevent the doomsday which he foresaw. I wondered where he'd hidden them, there had been no sign of them when I had gone through his things in Cadogan Street.

I sat stock still for a long time thinking about my father and his legacy. I resolved to find the mandalas and to complete his thesis and publish it in his memory. I would take the notebook home and show it to Polly and share it with her and together we would work on the project. After all, Polly more than anyone I knew would understand the importance of mandalas for illustrating my father's work.

Chapter 4

1

I drove down early on Friday morning for my meeting with Frank Waller at Southern Orchids, which was situated near Siddlesham on the Chichester Plain. I drove south from Horsham, through the flat land where the river Arun meanders, and up over the chalk downs at Houghton, then dropped down to the plain and turned west towards Chichester. It was a beautiful morning and the countryside looked wonderful, the ears on the crops of wheat and barley on either side of the bypass were just starting to emerge and rippled in the breeze.

During the drive I thought about the new clients I'd picked up during this first week since I had started my practise, and what a variety of occupations they had: an animal psychologist, a dentist, a scrap metal merchant, a second-hand bookshop and a dressmaker. The animal psychologist had been the most entertaining.

"It's not the dogs that need psychoanalysing", he said "it's the owners. They're the ones with all the mental problems. But they're the ones who pay!" and he roared with laughter at his own joke.

Southern Orchids was situated on the bypass within sight of the spire of Chichester cathedral and I turned into the entrance and parked in the visitors' car park outside the entrance to reception. At first sight it was a most impressive organisation, far bigger than I had imagined and everything was pristine and well-kept.

Frank was waiting for me inside the reception area and he came out to greet me. He looked fit and handsome, dressed in chinos and a short-sleeved green polo shirt with the Southern Orchids logo embroidered on the breast pocket.

Straight away Frank suggested that he should show me around the nursery and then we could deal with the paperwork and have a coffee.

First we saw the microprop unit as he called it. We had to don plastic overshoes, plastic overalls and a plastic hat, similar to a bath cap.

"We can't risk any contamination in here", he said "there's too much at stake".

The process of tissue culture was actually pretty straightforward as explained by Frank, and I saw each stage of production, from the laboratory where the minute pieces of plant tissue were cut from a meristem, through to their establishment in test tubes in a growth medium, to weaning and finally emerging as a plug or small rooted plant ready to be re-planted in compost and grown on in a traditional nursery environment.

"We're growing about three million plants a year now", said Frank, as we emerged from the microprop area and took off our plastic clothing and dumped it in a bin. "Now we'll have a look at the end products", and he led me through a succession of glasshouses. In each house there were plants larger than the previous one, and in the last three glasshouses there were mature plants ready to be shipped to customers when ordered. All these orchids were in square, white ceramic pots, staked and labelled and just starting to flower. The range of colours was breathtaking. Frank was visibly proud of his achievement.

"We're supplying most of the supermarkets now" said Frank, "we got an enquiry from Marks & Spencer about eighteen months ago and the others soon followed. It's driven our business forward very rapidly and now we have about six major customers, so we're no longer dependent on Robinsons although they get priority because they helped us to get started in the first place", he paused for breath, "now we'll just look into the sheds where we store the raw materials and pots and stuff, and mix the compost and I'll show you the machinery and equipment too. This will help to explain the items which you'll find in the books".

On the tour Frank introduced me to each member of staff. They all wore similar polo shirts to Frank, with the company logo. They were a friendly bunch of people, you could see they were well trained and knew exactly what they were supposed to be doing by their attitudes and obvious pride in the nursery and its products.

Back in the office I met the two women who were in charge of all the paperwork and accounts. We had coffee in Frank's office which doubled as a meeting room and had a large plasma screen at one end with a projector at the other. All the computers were modern and there was a large colour printer.

"We produce all our own publicity material and the website is kept up to date daily", said Frank. Just as he was asking me what I wanted to do next we were interrupted by the arrival of Frank's wife Kate and their two small children, Peter and Antonia. They were on their way to the beach for a picnic and had just looked in to see if Frank needed anything. Frank introduced me to his family. Kate was a typical Aussie, she looked healthy and strong and had an open face with fair hair, blue eyes and a broad smile. The kids were images of their parents, dressed in board shorts and T-shirts and obviously ready for action and reluctant to delay their visit to the beach. The three of them soon left. The office seemed very quiet once they'd gone.

"Now for the boring bit" I said, and I took Frank through the routine paperwork which was necessary for him to become a client.

I had prepared a set of papers for Frank to sign. These included a letter of engagement, details of my professional indemnity insurance, and forms for Frank to sign covering the money laundering regulations. As the business was incorporated as a limited company I asked Frank for a copy of the cerificate of incorporation and the articles of association. I'd already done a search at Companies House so I had copies of all the documents which had been filed. The whole thing took ten minutes.

"That wasn't too painful" said Frank "what next?"

"I'd like to agree the fees with you in advance if that's OK" I said " that'll mean I don't have to log all the time I spend and then argue the toss later".

"Good idea" replied Frank, "how much do you think it'll cost?"

"Well, Tim Berrington charged you five thousand a year for each of the last two years so I guess I can do it for the same amount", I said "the only reason for any change would be if there's something significant which needs special work done, in which case we can agree an additional fee before I do that extra work".

"Sounds good to me", said Frank and he extended his hand to shake mine. "Now let's go over to Ellie and Jake's place and I'll introduce you to them. I'll lead the way in my car if you like and then you can make your way home afterwards".

We said goodbye to the women in the office and drove out of the car park, Frank in his Saab and me following in my Mini Cooper.

As we drove along the bypass eastwards towards Haywards Heath I realised that I had grown to like Frank very much and to admire his energy and achievements. I remembered a warning which my senior at KPMG had constantly instilled in us: "Don't ever get emotionally involved with clients, it can blind you to reality". I resolved to stick to this mantra but it was going to be hard, there was something immensely attractive about Frank Waller.

We arrived at Jakellie Recycling which was still based at Frank's parents' old farm, although the business had by now taken over all the old farm buildings which had clearly been spruced up and modernised. Ellie and Jake were expecting us and gave me a warm welcome after they had kissed Frank. They offered us tea and biscuits but Frank declined, he had to get back to see the planners, he said.

After a cup of tea Ellie and Jake showed me round the business. It was much as Frank had already described it to me but there was considerable activity going on in the new machine shop, the business had recently expanded into repairing and renovating all kinds of machinery including quadbikes, motor mowers, chainsaws and other mechanical handtools.

The parts business also appeared to be thriving and during our tour of inspection a courier arrived to take a shipment of dozens of boxes and packages.

Later we sat in the office and went through the usual rigmarole of signing the papers, asking for various forms and details, and agreeing a fixed fee. I left Ellie and Jake to it and agreed to be in touch soon to arrange a date to start work on the annual accounts.

2

When I got home that evening Polly said "Dad wants you to ring him when you have a minute".

I went upstairs to have a wash and change my clothes and when I came back down I dialled Polly's parents' number.

"Hullo Adelbert", I said "it's Tom here. How are you?".

"Oh, Tom, thanks for calling back" said my father-in-law, "I'm fine thanks. I wondered if you would be prepared to do the audit of my Romanian charity, our accountant has just told us that he's going to retire at the end of next month?"

"Yes of course I will," I said without hesitating.

"Oh, thanks so much," he went on "I'll bring all the stuff down with me next Saturday, Polly's invited Camelia and me to stay the week-end".

"Great", I said "look forward to seeing you then," and I put down the phone. I felt rather pleased that Adelbert had asked me to do this for him. It was a priviledge to do something for my father-in-law and of course I wouldn't charge for the work, it was a way of making a contribution to his beloved charity. I went outside to look around the garden and I thought about Adelbert's work for the handicapped children in Romanian orphanages whose plight had been revealed in 1990 after Ceaucescu had been toppled.

As soon as it was possible to return to Romania Adelbert had gone to Bucharest several times to visit relatives and to investigate the situation in the orphanages for himself and to establish what they needed most in the way of supplies and equipment. As soon as he got back to England he had sat down with Camelia and they had drawn up a plan for the best way to help their compatriots.

Eventually Adelbert founded a charity which supported a number of orphanages, but to start with he had made a list of the most vital medical supplies which were needed, from medecines to dressings to bed linen to disposable nappies and a hundred and one other items. Then he had badgered all the suppliers of these items for gifts of certain things and when gifts weren't forthcoming he got them at cost price and paid for them himself or got donations of money from friends and colleagues.

As soon as he had a truck load of supplies he borrowed an old lorry from a friend with a removal business and he drove it all the way to Romania himself to save money and to ensure that everything reached the right place, sleeping for short periods in lay-byes along the route.

After the fall of the Ceaucescu regime Romania was in a desperate state, often without electricity and with few available items to purchase. There was plenty of help available but not many resources. For example, sewing machines were very scarce so that blankets and sheets and curtains and clothes were not able to be made although there were plenty of people ready to set to and make anything which was needed.

Without a reliable supply of electricity it wsn't possible to operate an electric sewing machine anyway, so Adelbert hit on the idea of getting hold of old treddle sewing machines and he put an advertisement in several British national newspapers. The response was phenomenal and he received nearly eight hundred machines, some of which needed repairing or servicing, which he stored in a disused engine shed owned by the railway. He quickly learnt the basics of how a treddle sewing machine operated and worked through the night fixing them up.

Next morning he was back at work in the hospital in Whitechapel. As soon as the sewing machines were servicable he got hold of thousands of reels of cotton and thread of any colour available and again transported everything to Bucharest in the removal van.

Slowly the orphanages came back to life and the children began to get better and the members of staff were able to plan the future with some certainty. Now, years later the charity had grown beyond all recognition and was run on professional lines and was able to support more and more orphanages.

3

Polly and I worked hard to get our smallholding into shape. We embraced country life in every way. We started a vegetable garden. Polly had green fingers and I had the experience of our old family allotment in Ealing, so we cleared the ground and mulched it and rotavated it and planted our first crops. We built a chicken run and bought a chook house and a dozen point-of-lay pullets from a nearby chicken farmer. We planted out the beds around the house with roses and potentillas and other flowering shrubs.

We bought all our equipment second-hand from Jakellie Recycling, a rotavator, a rotary mower, a chainsaw, a strimmer and other bits and pieces. Jake picked out suitable items for us and he and Ellie brought them over to Sedgwick Farm to demonstrate them and have a sticky beak at what we were up to.

We needed something to keep down the grass in the paddocks and a young couple who were local sheep farmers, Andy and Tracy Wilmot offered to keep a few lambs in the fields. Andy had a fencing business to supplement their income while they built up their flock so he quickly erected a stock-proof fence around the paddocks and laid on a permanent water supply.

Towards the end of August we started to flag a bit as a result of our efforts, so we decided to take a week's holiday to recharge our batteries. We needed to get right away. For several years Polly's brother Stefan had owned *Cinnabar Moth* a Contessa 26 yacht which had been built by Jeremy Rogers in Lymington. Stefan worked for an oil company and had just heard that he'd been posted to Norway to join a survey boat for a six months spell and he needed someone to keep an eye on *Cinnabar Moth* while he was away.

Stefan rented a berth in the marina at Hayling Island Sailing Club and gave the keys of the boat to Polly who promised to visit her regularly. We had been out several times for a day's sail and taken a picnic with us and explored Chichester Harbour before venturing out into the Solent. Now we decided to go for a week's sailing holiday, westward down Channel towards Land's End. Andy and Tracy offered to look after our place while we were away. We had a wonderful time and got as far as Falmouth, and returned refreshed and fit.

I spent the following week doing the accounts at Jakellie Recycling. The latest machine shop was housed in an old grain store and was entirely devoted to a new division of the business. This division had a contract to repair, restore and respray different types of machine owned by Golf GB which was a chain of about twenty-five golf clubs throughout the country. The nearest course to Jakellie was Cottesloe Golf and Country Club which was within a quarter of an hour's drive of Gatwick Airport. The person who owned Golf GB was Brazilian and he also owned a group of up-market country hotels.

"Another oligarch laundering money I suppose" I said, but Ellie and Jake protested.

"Pedro Vargas is a great guy", said Jake "and he's been very supportive ever since we got the contract. He pays on the nail too".

"We get a fixed fee for restoring and servicing the various machines, on a sliding scale", said Ellie. "These range from golf carts, to quad bikes, mowers, chainsaws and strimmers".

Jake had developed a couple of clever ideas which not only speeded up the servicing process but also saved money. One was an oil filtration system which recycled engine oil and removed all of the impurities from the oil so that it could be used again. Jake had also devised a paint-sprayer which was controlled by a digital camera and a computer and which automatically followed the contours of each machine and this avoided the necessity of masking the parts of the machine which were not being sprayed. All the machines which had been restored looked as good as new.

I didn't have to do a stocktake for this part of the business because the machines were the property of Golf GB and were therefore not owned by Jakellie.

Ellie mentioned that she was very much involved with amateur dramatics in the town and produced plays and acted in small cameo parts. Jake helped with the lighting and scenery, so this activity got them away from the business which otherwise might have become an obsession.

"I'll send you a couple of tickets for *The Cherry Orchard* as soon as they're printed, said Ellie "it's our most ambitious production for a long time. My friend Tina is playing the part of Mme Ranevskaya, she's sensational, we're hoping that one of the directors of The Old Vic is coming to see it and will fall in love with Tina and whisk her off to the West End and we'll see her name in lights!"

Jake grunted something and went into the stores to find a spare part.

"He's so jealous of the idea of Tina going to London", said Ellie "I think he's rather keen on her but nothing ever seems to happen between them." She sighed rather wistfully, she clearly wished her brother could find a romantic attachment.

I called out "Goodbye!" to Jake and said "see you soon" to Ellie, then I left and drove back home, thinking about the Wallers. The warning voice of my senior rang in my ears but I ignored it. Why shouldn't I like my clients, I thought.

When I got home I was set on by Pinky and Perky our two Jack Russell bitches. Polly appeared at the door.

"Don't be fooled by them", she said "I've taken them for two long walks already today". She looked at me in an odd way.

"What's up?" I asked.

"Well", she said, "let me see now. I've rebottled the elderflower cordial, picked all the runner beans, written two more of the educational papers, cooked your supper – oh and by the way I'm pregnant".

She blushed with joy and took a step towards me. I held her tightly for a very long time.

"Have you told your mother?" I asked.

"Not yet", she replied "I thought you should be the first to know, I'll ring her in a minute".

"Let's celebrate," I said "there's a bottle of champagne in the fridge just waiting for this, we could drink it outside and have supper outside too".

We sat and watched the sun go down behind the wood, there were a few clouds around the sun which made it a far more beautiful sunset than it would have been in just a clear sky. It was at times like this that I wished I could paint. I looked at Polly and she winked at me. I felt happier at that moment than I had ever felt in my life.

4

One of the rules attaching to a practising certificate was that each year you had to undertake a certain number of hours of 'continued professional education', or CPE as it was known. This could either be achieved by attending lectures on the latest changes in regulations, or by reading up on these. Most people did a bit of both. Each year you had to complete a return for the Institute confirming thet you had complied with the rules.

I had received a circular from the local Society which announced that the autumn season of CPE lectures was to take place this year at Cottesloe Golf Club. The opening session was to include a tour of the club's facilities followed by light refreshments; afterwards there would be a talk on 'Risk evaluation in audits' by a well-known lecturer from The London Business School. Guests were welcome. It was clearly a promotional exercise for Cottesloe Golf Club to demostrate its new conference facilities. I decided to go and Polly said she'd like to come along too.

Cottesloe's facilities were pretty impressive. They had a heated indoor swimming pool, a gymn, squash and badminton courts, and a number of function rooms. Most of these had views over the course which looked immaculate. The cctv control room was the biggest surprise. There were about thirty-five screens, each one for a camera focussed on a green or a tee or part of a fairway or on the buildings. They were in high definition so that you could watch anything which was in view. It was rather like the Camera Obscura at Aberystwith.

The light lunch was a choice of various home-cooked finger foods. There was no alcohol, only soft drinks. It was low-key but just right. Afterwards we attended the lecture which was mercifully short and very much to the point.

"There are dozens of complicated fomulae available for assessing the risks attached to auditing a business", said the lecturer, "these risks include the involvement of the owners, the management structure of the business, the amount of cash included in the turnover, the internal controls and so on". He paused.

"You know about these already", he said, "but how do you actually tackle the work?" He paused again, then he took a black felt-tipped marker pen and drew a large circle on the white board on the wall behind him.

"This represents all of the transactions for a year", he said. Then he drew a small segment on the edge of the circle. "These are the really big transactions. Check all of these thoroughly", then he drew a second small segment, "these are the 'funny' or unusual transactions. Check all of these thoroughly too. Then check ten percent of all the rest", he paused for a third time.

"That's all", he said, "any questions?".

Polly was pleasantly surprised by the lecturer's performance. She said she'd understood every word. She was particularly impressed by his use of a diagram to get his point across.

As there were no questions, the chairman gave us details of the next meeting. At this moment Pedro Vargas appeared and stood in front of the audience. He was tall and urbane, with thick slightly wavy dark hair and amazing white teeth. He wore an Armani pale grey suit with a cream shirt open at the collar. He looked just like a Hollywood star.

"Welcome to Cottesloe", he said, "I hope you've enjoyed your visit. I just want to say that we are pleased to offer a specially discounted membership of the club to all those who have been here today. You may join as golfing members or as social members, and whichever you choose you are welcome to use all of the club's facilities at any time." He paused for a few seconds.

"To help you decide, we shall be pleased for you to become honorary members for one month from today, just pick up a leaflet from the desk at the back of the room and complete it before you go. Now, pease enjoy a cup of tea or coffee before you leave".

He stepped off the dais and started to mingle with the crowd.

"What a smoothie", said Polly, "he's just like Zoltan Karpathy, oozing charm from every pore he oiled his way around the floor".

She was slightly caught off guard to find him at her elbow as she finished speaking. He turned on the charm.

"Do you play golf?" he asked.

"No, actually my husband and I don't play, but we very much enjoy walking with our dogs", she replied, recovering her poise.

"What sort of dogs are they?" enquired Pedro.

"Jack Russells", replied Polly.

"Ah, my favourite breed", said Pedro, then confidentially "please feel free to walk them on the course whenever you like, provided of course they don't interfere with the players or pinch their golf balls!", and he smiled his dazzling smile and moved cat-like on to his next target.

"There you are", I said "he's not so bad as you thought, and it might make a change to walk here occasionally".

"Hm", said Polly, "I still wouldn't touch him with a barge pole", she looked thoughtful, "come on, let's go home now".

Chapter 5

1

I stared at the schedule and went through my calculations for the umpteenth time. It just didn't add up. I stood up and walked around Frank's office at Southern Orchids, trying to see where I had made my mistake. Then I sat down again at his table and rearranged all the relevant documents in order. Frank had let me use his room because he was away for a few days at an International Plant Propagators' Society conference in Germany.

I went through the schedule step-by-step one more time.

Opening stock of rooting containers *plus* purchases *less* sales should *equal* closing stock, give or take a small allowance for breakages and other losses. But the difference was one and a half million rooting containers. At a cost of thirty-five pence a container that came to a short-fall of more than half a million pounds. It was far too large to ignore.

The rooting containers were purpose-made plastic containers in which the plants grown by tissue culture changed from being in-vitro plugs into proper rooted plants similar to plants which had been propagated from seed or cuttings.

After I had been appointed by Frank as auditor to Southern Orchids I had made a study of micropropagation so that I could understand what I should expect to find in the books and accounts. It was quite a complex business and I asked Polly to prepare a diagram to illustrate the activities and flows of materials, from the preparation of the tiny explants in growing media inside test tubes right through to the saleable plants in retail containers.

Polly's diagram was a triumph of clarity and detail and showed not only the progress of a plant from woe to go but every item of equipment and material needed for the process. In due course the diagram became a standard part of the course for practically every department of botany in UK universities and colleges.

I glanced at my watch. Four o'clock. I decided to go home and have tea and chill out. I put all the stuff in my case, said goodnight to the office staff and drove home.

When I got home I changed and made a pot of tea and sat down in the kitchen with Polly and told her about the difference I had discovered at Southern Orchids. I showed her the schedule.

"Are you sure the stock numbers are correct?" she said.

"Yes, I checked the physical stock sheets with the computer print-outs and they agree exactly. I double checked all the purchases too, and I got all the suppliers to confirm their deliveries for the year. Everything tallied".

"Then the problem must be in the sales", said Polly, "either that or someone's stolen a whole lot of rooting containers".

"I'll have to wait until Frank gets back and go through it with him", I said, "apart from this one item everything is in apple pie order".

"So now you can put it on the back burner and get on with planning for the Round the Island Race in *Cinnabar Moth* on Saturday. We need to be on board by Friday afternoon so as to be ready at Cowes for the start at six o'clock on Saturday morning. Andy and Tracy are staying here for the week-end so we can get away nice and early".

There was plenty to do to get ready for the famous annual race round the Isle of Wight. There would be literally hundreds of yachts taking part and the starting guns for each class of yacht would be at intervals of ten minutes, so it was vital to be in place and not miss one's slot.

I needed to study the sailing instructions issued by The Island Sailing Club carefully and look at the tide charts and decide whether to take the island side or the mainland side as we headed westwards and out through the Needles. Polly would be on the tiller and I would look after the sails and man the foredeck. I completely forgot about the problem at Southern Orchids for the rest of the week-end.

2

We actually got aboard *Cinnabar Moth* just after lunchtime on the Friday. There was plenty to do before we left the marina. We had to top up the diesel tank, test the motor and charge the batteries. We had to fill the fresh water tanks and check the GPS and the navigation system and all the lights.

We took the sails out of their bags and gave them an airing whilst we were replacing the genoa sheets with new ones which Stefan had ordered. We replaced the battens on the mainsail with new battens which had been delivered with the genoa sheets.

We stowed all our food and provisions and clothing in the lockers on board and put the empty bags and containers back in the car. We made a quick mug of tea and sat looking across the water towards the Winner sand bank and beyond into the Channel.

There were puffy white clouds moving fast above a choppy sea and the force four wind was catching the stays and halyards of all the yachts on the marina so that there was a constant metallic noise as they rattled against the masts. Eventually we hoisted the main and set sail, passed the foreland at Hayling and crossed over to Cowes, sailing close to Horse Sand Fort.

We found a place alongside some other Contessas on Cowes Roads' swinging moorings which are additional rows of deepwater moorings especially for visiting yachtsmen which are laid to the north of the Shrape Breakwater usually from June through to September. Our neighbour was another Contessa 26 called *Firefly* and the owner knew Stefan well so he was most friendly to Polly and me when we explained who we were.

The following morning we were awake at dawn and after eating a banana and some biscuits we got all our sails out ready and motored down to be near the start. The wind had died away during the night and was only about force two with a nasty drizzle and poor visibility.

A couple of minutes before our ten minute gun was due we cut the engine and hoisted the main. At the five minute gun we hoisted the genoa and tried to work our way along to the windward end of the starting line. We had decided to tack over to the mainland shore, so we weren't too bothered about being right at the front of the pack at the start as long as we were at the windward end. Bang went the starting gun and we came round into the wind and immediately tacked to starboard to get away from the main fleet and over towards the mainland.

To start with the race was little more than a drifting match but because there was more tide under us along the mainland shore we emerged in the front group of Contessas when we got to the Needles where the wind strenthened to about force four and allowed us to turn south-east and reach down to St Catherine's Point with our spinnaker set.

I made us some sandwiches and mugs of tea and we sat together in the cockpit. It was quite warm by now and the boat flew along in the stiff breeze, surging down each wave as it picked up *Cinnabar Moth* and pushed her forward. It was exciting to look aft and see each wave bearing down on us and then pass under the hull.

After rounding St Catherine's, Polly took us on a direct course past Ventnor and Shanklin and when we reached Bembridge Ledge we handed the spinnaker again and tacked back up the east Solent with the genoa set, to the finishing line at Cowes. It had taken us just over ten hours to complete the course and we came fourth of the nine Contessa 26 yachts which finished.

The best thing about the race was that we had become much more confident sailing together and felt that we would be able to do some cruising on our own in the future and nip over to France and explore some of the coastline of Normandy and Brittany.

We decided not to go ashore at Cowes for the prize-giving but instead we turned eastwards and sailed slowly back to Chichester Harbour and our berth at Hayling where we cleaned up and stowed the sails and locked up the boat and drove home. Andy and Tracy had left by the time we got in but we got a boisterous welcome from Pinky and Perky.

"East west home's best", said Polly and grinned at me. Pregnancy suited her and the wind and sun had tanned her already sallow skin so that she looked more than ever like a gypsy.

3

I spent the following week doing the audit of The Chaotic Scrap Metal and Recycling Company Limited at Broadbridge Heath. This was the place where Jake Waller got his moped parts from. In actual fact the business was far from chaotic and I soon discovered that Charlie Farley, the owner, made lots of brass from muck, by knowing how to extract every bit of value from the items which he bought at a flat rate per tonne from the people who wanted to get rid of them. It was an amazingly profitable business from the owner's point of view.

However, there were a couple of major problems from my point of view. First, practically every transaction was for cash so that it was difficult to know whether the books represented the whole picture. Second, the value of the stock at the end of the accounting year was arbitrary to say the least. I decided to broach these problems with Charlie before spending any more time on looking at the details.

"Yeah", said Charlie "that's the reason why my last auditors gave me the push. They said they couldn't verify everything. What do you want to do? I gotta have the books audited or the tax people will be round my neck".

"You're VAT registered", I said, "who does your VAT return every quarter?"

"The wife", replied Charlie. He looked at me through his dark glasses which he wore even when he was indoors, even when he was inside a cupboard looking for something, so that it wasn't possible to see into his eyes. He had a rather world-weary look and a nervous tick.

"Do you want the wife to come up here to go through the stuff with you?" he asked.

"Yes, of course", I answered, "when could she do that?"

For an answer Charlie got out his iPhone and pressed a button.

"Peg love, can you come to the office please" he said. A few minutes later an enormous tractor with a telescopic grab drove up and parked in the yard outside the office door and a woman in blue dungarees climbed down from the cab and came through the door. She was quite the largest woman I had seen for a long time. She wiped away some stray strands of blond hair which were floating in front of her eyes and held out a greese-stained hand.

"How d'you do love" she said, "you must be the new auditor", then without pausing "my real name's Peggy but I got sick of being called Piggy Malone so please call me Peg. Let's make a cup of tea and we can sit down and have a look through everything".

"I'll make the tea", volunteered Charlie, and he wandered off into the kitchen.

The VAT returns were in good shape and tallied with the print-outs from the accounts. So far so good. All the documents were in date order and represented all the transactions in the VAT return, whether for cash or cheques or payments and receipts by credit card and on-line. Still so far so good. The gross profit was consistent at about forty percent. Good.

I asked Peg to prepare a list of all the balances in the bank accounts and savings accounts and any other kinds of instruments, including actual cash of course, plus the stock at the year-end.

While she was doing this I worked out the equivalent totals at the start of the year. Then I calculated how much net cash the business had generated during the year. The opening balances plus the surplus should add up to the closing balances. And amazingly they did.

"Everything goes through the books", said Peg, "it's just not worth while trying to fiddle anything, I couldn't sleep at night", and she looked disarmingly at me.

I wondered how she had managed to fiddle it. She was cetainly a brilliant bookkeeper. Ah well, as long as they signed a disclaimer stating that everything was included in the accounts and that nothing had been omitted, why should I worry?

But of course I did worry, and I puzzled away at the problem all that week.

4

One evening I drove home from The Chaotic Scrap Metal and Recycling Company Limited through torrential rain with heavy winds buffetting the car. The visibility was poor and I drove very slowly. There were several branches lying in the road and twice I had to stop the car and drag one on to the verge. It was a relief to get home safely and to park the car and run through the rain to the back door and into the warm kitchen.

During supper Polly told me about her adventure on Cottesloe Golf Course.

"I went for a walk on the golf course early this morning just after you'd left for the scrapyard", she said. "I took Pinky and Perky and I wore my sailing gear, waterproofs and a sou'wester, and my wellies". She paused to help herself to some more vegetables.

"It was pretty bracing but good fun and there weren't any golfers around which meant the dogs could be off the lead. When we reached the northern end of the course Pinky and Perky chased a rabbit into some thick undergrowth and disappeared. I tried to get them to come back but they took no notice of my shouting and whistling so in the end I had to struggle through the thick undergrowth to try and get them."

"Suddenly I found myself up against a high chain link fence with both razor wire and an electrified wire along the top and every few yards a yellow sign with 'High Voltage! Danger keep out!' in black letters. I looked through the fence down into a disused stone quarry and guess what I saw?"

"Tell me", I said.

"About a third of the area of the quarry was covered over with five Buckminster-Fuller style geodesic domes made of glass, similar to those we saw at the Eden Project near Bodelva in Cornwall. There's a very modern building which looks like a laboratory next to the domes, and just inside the entrance to the quarry site is a really huge agricultural-style building."

"There were fork-lift trucks bringing shrink-wrapped pallets out of the building and loading them into two large trucks with curtains drawn back at the sides. The area was floodlit like a football stadium although the day was getting brighter".

"Go on", I said, intrigued.

"Well I noticed that that someone or something had burrowed under the chain-link fence so I guessed that's where Pinky and Perky had probably got through into the quarry area. I wriggled through the gap and soon found the dogs, covered in mud, emerging from a rabbit hole. I put them on their leads, then I wriggled back under the fence again and we walked quickly home for breakfast".

After supper we got out the Ordnance Survey map. The quarry was clearly marked but there were no signs of any buildings or domes, although it was the latest edition of the map. We switched on a computer and looked at Google Earth but again there was absolutely no sign of anything in the quarry. It was a complete mystery.

"Well you'll have to come with us when we go for a walk next time and see for yourself", said Polly as we were doing the washing up, and I agreed that I would.

We actually didn't get an opportunity to walk on the golf course for quite a while because we were so busy at home, so we just gave Pinky and Perky a quick run every now and then around our own paddocks.

5

Towards the end of that week Polly received an email to tell her that the publishing company which was using her diagram articles had gone bust.

"What a bummer", said Polly "just as I was getting into the swing of it and they seemed to like my articles so much. I wonder what went wrong. Oh well, I suppose I can always go back to work as a free-lancer".

"Why not join me in the practice?" I asked, "I've got so many new clients now I could really do with someone to work with me. Besides, you could do whatever hours you choose and work at home when the baby arrives. What do you think?"

"But I don't know nearly enough about accountancy", she replied.

"Maybe not just now," I said "but you could soon learn the ropes and there are masses of opportunities to redesign schedules and develop new diagrams to give clients better information. And it's always a help to have someone to talk things over with. Why not give it a trial, you can always stop if you decide you're not enjoying it. I've got to get someone to help me and there's no-one I'd rather have than you".

Polly sat staring at the road ahead. She was frowning as she always did when she was puzzling something out.

"OK", she suddenly said "we'll give it a go".

Chapter 6

1

I rang Frank Waller the following Monday, after he had returned from Germany, and I mentioned the discrepancy in the stocks of rooting containers.

"Oh, I can explain that when I see you", he said. "Kate and I were wondering if you and Polly would like to come over to our place next Saturday for a barbecue lunch and to have a look at our new home?"

"That'd be good," I said "thanks very much, what time?"

"About midday if that's OK", replied Frank, "I'll email you with the address and details of how to find us. Look forward to seeing you then", and he rang off.

Polly and I put the finishing touches to our new bathroom during the evenings of that week. We had installed a power shower over the bath and a new wash basin, bidet and WC. Then we tiled the floor and the walls and painted the ceiling. I did the plumbing and Polly stuck on the tiles and grouted them, while I cut any tiles which needed altering and painted the ceiling. It looked half decent when we'd finished.

"Now for the new kitchen", said Polly, "and then we'd better do up the nursery". She was starting to look quite pregnant now but was still very fit and mobile. I knew she wouldn't slow up just because she was having a baby, all I could do was help as much as I could.

We drove over to the Wallers' new home on Saturday morning. Beale House was a magnificent old Georgian house covered in wisteria and climbing roses. There were flint sheds and outhouses and a meadow running down to the water beyond a ha-ha, with a boathouse up a small creek on one side of the grass.

After being shown round the house and going for a stroll down to the water's edge, we sat in deck chairs on the lawn and sipped elderflower cordial and mineral water while Frank cooked sausages and lamb cutlets on the barbecue. Frank and Kate were both teetotal and Polly and I were happy to go along with that. We ate the meat with green salad and asparagus, followed by raspberries and cream. The two children, Peter and Antonia, ate their lunch up quickly and went off down to the boathouse together.

After we'd all cleared away the lunch things Frank suggested that I might like to have a look at his latest project which was about ten minutes away by car. Kate wanted to show Polly some baby clothes and bits of equipment which she thought Polly might like for our baby when it arrived, so Frank and I went off in his car.

As we drove along Frank told me that he was at last realising his dream of creating an English tree nursery, on a fifty acre site near Emsworth, in partnership with Chichester College. Frank was leasing the site from Chichester County Council and had designed the whole project which was to be used as a horticultural unit for third-year students as an actual hands-on commercial enterprise, "From seed to sale", as Frank put it. He drove up to the metal security gate and pressed a button on his car key ring and the gate slid open to allow Frank to drive through it. We got out of the car and Frank sketched out his plan.

The tree nursery would be a huge outfit when it was completed and would have several novel features, including water-saving devices, solar heating, and use recycled materials wherever possible. Schools throughout the area would be involved in the enterprise, being presented with packets of seeds and instructions for germinating them so that a network of young people will provide seedlings for the nursery and eventually also be involved with planting the trees.

"The target is to produce up to half a million seedlings a year when the development is complete", said Frank.

"Where are you going to get all the seeds from?" I asked Frank.

"Well, we've created a network of seed-gatherers through local Scouts and Guides and Cubs and Brownies and Beavers" he replied. "The Millenium Seed Bank at Wakehurst Place will supply us with instructions on how and when to gather seeds and store them and we'll distribute these with containers and labels. It's vital that we know the provenance and location of every seed we collect so that the seedlings can be returned to the same area to be planted in due course. The collecting groups will carry out their work in the autumn each year and we'll clean and sort them ready to distribute them to the schools for germinating in the following spring. If successful we'll franchise the scheme throughout the country. It'll be quite an operation", he said.

What an understatement, I thought.

"Now, let me show you around", said Frank.

The site had been cleared and the positions of the proposed glasshouses had been pegged out, and a borehole had been drilled to provide water for the nursery, the valves and pipes were on the surface in the centre of the site. A reservoir was next to the borehole where all the rain and surplus water from the bore would be collected.

"We're also going to instal a ground source heat pump to provide heating for the glasshouses and the office block and potting sheds, using the same borehole, it goes down a hundred and twenty meters", said Frank.

He showed me where the paths and roadways would be installed and how he planned to install various methods of irrigation so that students could decide which worked best in different circumstances. I was pretty impressed by the scale of the enterprise and the vision that was creating it.

On the way back to Beale House Frank suddenly said:

"Did you know that Ellie's disappeared again?"

Apparently this had happened several times during the past year but she'd always come back. No explanation, no apparent problem or cause. Each time Jake's been frantic with worry that there's something wrong with Ellie but she's never even hinted at the reason.

"I wonder what on earth she's up to", I said " is it something to do with am-dram or is she tied up with some man?"I asked.

"We haven't a clue" said Frank "but whatever it is, this time she's been gone for nearly a week with no sign or contact from her. She left her mobile phone behind at Jackellie Recycling and she hasn't used her credit card". I sat silently thinking about the possible reasons for her disappearance.

"Jake's beside himself with worry, and besides he's having to do all the paperwork as well as his usual jobs", says Frank, "can you have a look at the books to see if you can find anything which would give us a clue as to where or why she's gone?".

Of course I said I'd drop everything and go over on Monday morning. I quite forgot to ask Frank about the stock problem at Southern Orchids and besides, when I did remember on the way home it seemed rather unimportant compared with Ellie's disappearance.

When I told Polly about Ellie she said she would come with me to see if she could help to throw some light on the mystery.

2

Jake was expecting Polly and me when we arrived at Jakellie Recycling on Monday morning. He brewed up some tea and coffee and we sat discussing Ellie's disappearance with him. Jake's eyes were red and he looked as if he'd had very little sleep for quite some time.

"Have you been in touch with the Police?" asked Polly.

Jake took off his gunmetal-rimmed spectacles and wiped the lenses on his handkerchief. He blinked at Polly.

"No," he said "I haven't". He seemed to go into a sort of reverie for what seemed a long time.

"Look," he said "it isn't a case of abduction or anything like that. She's come back quite OK each time she's disappeared, and carried on with her work and everything else absolutely normally. I just can't interfere in her life. If she wants to go off now and then it's entirely up to her. It's the uncertainty that's the problem, and all the extra work I have to do when she's not here. The contract with Golf GB is spiralling out of control – we're getting all their stuff to service from every golf course in the area now and they're in the process of taking over the management of a dozen more courses". He blinked at Polly again.

"Would you like us to look through the books to see if we can come up with a clue as to where she is?", asked Polly.

"Oh no thanks", replied Jake "dear old Frank he's too much of a control-freak, I expect he told you to do that. There's nothing here that will give us a clue where Ellie's gone. Look, it's very good of you to come over but I just have to sit this thing out and carry on the business until Ellie comes back. Don't worry about me please. Look, I've really got to get on now, thanks very much for coming", and he stood up to indicate that he wanted us to leave.

We drove off and decided to go straight to Southern Orchids to bring Frank up-to-date and to tell him about our visit to Jakellie Recycling.

"Of course Jake's not telling us the whole story", said Polly as soon as we were on the bypass, "he knows jolly well where Ellie is but he's not letting on to us".

"How on earth do you know that?" I asked.

"Well he's not nearly worried enough about Ellie to start with, if he were he'd have got in touch with the missing persons department of the police, and I think he's covering up for her. I also sensed a bit of a rift or at least a difference of opinion between him and Frank, from what he said about Frank being a control-freak".

I didn't disagree with Polly. She had a sixth sense when it came to this sort of thing. Ever since she'd joined me in the practice she'd shown an uncanny ability to get to the bottom of tricky problems. She had a holistic way of looking at the world instead of the rather narrow view which an accountant or other professional might have. She'd already uncovered several cans of worms in clients' businesses which I had completely overlooked in spite of - or maybe because of - my rigorous and disciplined training at KPMG.

Frank was waiting for us when we got to Southern Orchids.

"How'd you get on with Jake?" he asked as soon as we got into his office.

"Nothing to report", said Polly, "he's soldiering on as usual, waiting for Ellie to come back".

"Ah well", said Frank "maybe she'll turn up soon". He looked worried.

"Would this be a good time to discuss the stock difference?" I asked, trying to change the subject and to move the conversation away from the Ellie affair.

Frank frowned. Then he looked up and smiled. He poured us out some coffee.

"Why not", he said, "are you sitting comfortably? Then I'll begin".

3

"About eighteen months ago I had a call from Pedro Vargas", said Frank. "Pedro told me that he'd heard about Southern Orchids from a mutual friend at Robinsons and he wondered if he could come over and have a look around. I saw no reason to say no so we arranged a date and he came over. We were just in the final stages of our development and the place was rather frenetic but Pedro seemed genuinely interested so I took time to show him everything. He was especially interested in the microprop unit".

Frank paused to see if we were still with him, then he went on.

"Afterwards Pedro asked me if he could take me out to lunch and as it was after midday I thought why not, I've got to eat and it's a good way of getting rid of him anyway. Over lunch Pedro told me a bit about himself and the fact that he had founded a charity back home in Brazil which was trying to save the rainforest from any more devastation. Well this was right up my street as you know, so I sat up and really paid attention to what he had to say."

"It seems that the charity has three prongs, the first of which is to bring about awareness of the potential damage to the world's climate by deforestation, by educating people and by lobbying all kinds of influential people to bring pressure to bear on the loggers and global corporations who want to clear the trees and plant oil palms and suchlike. The second prong is to create a fund to be used to recompense the people who own or inhabit the rainforest and to make it more worthwhile to leave the trees to grow rather than to cut them down, and the third prong is to try and re-establish the rainforest by planting more trees of the varieties which have been cut down".

Frank paused again. He poured us some more coffee and some water for himself.

"Pedro then told me that there are several species of trees and shrubs which are threatened with extinction in Brazil, one in particular. He asked me if we could propagate a largeish batch of this plant by tissue culture if he could get hold of some suitable material, so I said we'd give it a go. He asked me which part of the plant would be the best for an operation like this, so I told him and drew him a sketch of the sorts of bits which provide the best meristems for micropropagation. Pedro then asked me how much we'd charge for a weaned plant – the charity would pay for everything – and I said that each plug would cost about a quid, and how many did he think he'd want".

Frank drank some more water from his glass and put it down on the table reflectively. He smiled to himself as he remembered the conversation.

"What d'you think his reply was?" he asked, and then without waiting for us to answer he said "anything between one and two million plants".

"What did you say?" asked Polly.

"Well, I gulped a bit and then I said that would be fine. Pedro looked very relieved and he went up to the counter in the restaurant and paid the bill and we shook hands and parted company"

"Then what happened?" I asked.

"Well, I'd forgotten all about it to be honest, and then about a couple of months later Pedro turned up at the nursery out of the blue with a metal flask a bit like a thermos and unscrewed the lid and took out a big piece of plant wrapped in moist spontex and handed it to me. I unwrapped it carefully and examined it. It was perfect for the job. Pedro asked me to propagate as many plants as possible and said that he would pay me half a million euros up front to cover the initial cost".

Frank smiled again.

"Pedro went out to his car and reappeared with a soft leather bag, you know one of those Louis Vuitton things which very rich people take on board planes as hand luggage. He put it on the table – right there where the coffee pot is now – and unzipped it and took out a thousand new €500 notes. Then he went back to his car and drove off".

Frank went on "It actually proved quite easy to grow plants from the material Pedro had provided and in the event we grew about a million and a half pretty good weaned plants. Naturally I didn't want to touch the cash until I'd finished the contract, so I stuck the case with the money in an old steel shipping container where I keep all the really valuable stuff and any chemicals for the nursery, I showed it to you when I first took you round, it's in one of the potting sheds. Pedro came to collect the plants with a couple of huge trucks so that they could be packed up and shipped to Brazil. He gave me two more Louis Vuitton cases each with half a million euros in them in €500 notes, then he shook my hand and said "Nice to do business with you Frank. Don't spend it all at once!" and he went off in the truck sitting next to the driver in the cab, as happy as Larry".

"So that's where the stock of containers went", said Polly. "What've you done with the cash?"

"That's the problem," said Frank "I just don't know what to do about it all. The cash is still in the cases in the steel container, I'm a million and a half containers short and yet I just don't feel like touching the money. Besides, Kate thinks that €500 notes are mostly used for money-laundering and may not even be legal tender in Britain anyway and she doesn't think I should have had anything to do with Pedro Vargas, she says she wouldn't touch him with a barge pole, he gives her the creeps."

"Isn't that exactly what I said at the Cottesloe meeting?" said Polly.

"Well, we've got to think of a way of dealing with the transaction in your books", I said, "Polly and I will talk it over and come up with a couple of suggestions. We can't just ignore it". Frank nodded.

"What did the plants look like?" asked Polly.

Frank went out of the room for a minute and returned with a small bushy plant in a conventional plastic pot. It looked a bit like a camellia. He handed it to Polly and told her to keep it as a souvenir.

"I've got a few more", he said "it's semi-tropical so don't plant it in a frost hollow".

4

We had a good crowd staying at our place for a house-warming party the following week-end: Polly's brothers Stefan and Angelo who had been sailing in a regatta at Hayling Island in *Cinnabar Moth*, my cousin Toby Hartridge, Alex Frenkel and his new American girl friend Jeannie, and Andy and Tracy Wilmot who had helped us so much ever since we moved in to Sedgwick Farm.

We ate mostly barbecues and the weather was glorious, it was just after the longest day, so we spent nearly all the time out of doors. We had set up a badminton court on the lawn and a very 'local rules' croquet pitch as well so there was plenty to do.

The time flew by and the house seemed very empty when everyone left on Sunday afternoon after tea.

"That Jeannie is an interesting person", said Polly when we were washing up together, "she worked for Microsoft in Seattle after she got her degree in computer science at Washington State University. Now she has her own business looking after people's IT installations and she can service their systems remotely from her own computer, she showed me how she does it".

"She and Alex seem to get on well", I said "do you think they'll move in together?"

"Jeannie tells me they already have", said Polly, "they were made for each other. Alex is much more on the ball than he used to be, Jeannie is very good for him. He's recently got a top job in some ministry or other, she didn't say which".

The following Wednesday we went back to Cottesloe for another CPE meeting. This time the guest speaker was none other than Troy Patton from the US whose subject was 'How to build a five million dollar practice'. I'd heard of Troy and was quite intrigued to hear his schpeel. He was billed as the Tom Peters of the accountancy world.

Part way through Troy's presentation Polly had to slip out of the conference to go to the lavatory. The baby was getting quite big by now and Polly found that she needed to pee more frequently than before. She slipped out of the hall and walked along the corridor. She passed a maid who was cleaning the floor with a mop. The maid looked up as Polly passed her, she had black hair and was wearing a headscarf. Polly looked straight into the maid's eyes. It was Ellie.

Before Polly had time to say anything Ellie put her finger up to her lips and motioned Polly to go on walking to the toilets at the end of the corridor. She picked up her mop and bucket and walked along behind Polly. There was nobody else inside the lavatory.

"Whisper!" said Ellie in a very quiet whisper herself, then she turned the taps on in one of the basins. She put her mouth right up to Polly's ear, "don't say anything to anybody about this. I plan to be back at Jakellie on Thursday night, can you and Tom be there at eight o'clock, then I can tell you and Jake what I've been up to?"

"Yes, of course", breathed Polly. Ellie turned off the taps, flushed one of the toilets and disappeared with her mop and bucket. Polly did a pee, washed her hands and returned to the lecture hall. There was no sign of Ellie in the corridor.

After Troy had finished his talk there were the usual questions followed by coffee and bsicuits. When we got back to our car and were driving out of the car park Polly told me about her encounter with Ellie.

"What on earth is she doing there?" I wondered.

"Ask no questions and you'll be told no lies", said Polly, but I could tell she was just as intrigued as I was.

We went back to the office to finalise the accounts of the animal psychologist. He had earned some substantial fees as an expert witness in several high profile court cases during the year, and had also been summoned to Buckingham Palace to give advice to The Queen on the behavioural problems of a couple of the royal corgies. He was always very discrete and never talked about his clients but I gained the impression that he thought some of them were pretty odd, to say the least.

5

"I got more and more suspicious that there was something fishy going on with the Golf GB contract", said Ellie when we met up the following evening at Jakellie Recycling, "it had grown way beyond the level which you could expect from servicing the equipment from just twenty-five golf courses, so I decided to do a bit of detective work".

Jake took off his spectacles and blew on the lenses and rubbed them with his cleaning cloth. He blinked at Ellie. She went on:

"When we started Jackellie, right at the start, Jake decided to attach an electronic chip to each piece of equipment before we shipped it out. We bought a batch of the chips which are used in sheep ear tags – we got the idea from Andy Wilmot who introduced us to a big sheep farmer on the Romney Marshes. He arranged for us to register our own personal identity number, just like a flock number, with consecutive individual numbers on each chip for each item of equipment."

"Jake brazed a chip on to a metal part of each item and tested the reader and up-loaded the details on to his laptop. This meant that we could identify any piece of machinery which came back to us or which we had to do anything with in the future".

Ellie paused for a moment to gather her thoughts.

"A friend of mine from school runs a contract cleaning business and she told me she'd just got the contract to clean the whole of the Cottesloe Club facilities. This was a major contract for her and she told me her manager was busy recruiting staff. I got dressed up in one of my black wigs and a costume from Les Miserables and went along and applied for a job, most of the staff are only part-time so as to keep the tax and national insurance bills to a minimum, so I had no difficulty in getting a job."

"I said I was from Slovakia and my papers hadn't come through yet and nobody seemed to care about it. They also offered to let me stay in the staff quarters at Cottesloe until I found a permanent place".

"Most of the cleaning takes place after hours. On the third evening I was there I got posted to the office section on the second floor which has very tight security. Once inside the office I was able to watch the cctv screens which show views from cameras all around the course by day, but there are several channels and that night they showed different views and they were focussed on activity in what looked like a disused quarry."

"Machines and equipment were being loaded onto pallets inside a huge warehouse and then shrink-wrapped before being taken outside on forklifts and then hoisted into trucks. As each truck was filled and drove out of the compound I could see they had the same name on the outside curtain NOWAKOWSKI Kraków Malopolski. There must have been at least ten trucks altogether".

"Could you tell whether any of the stuff on the pallets came from here?" asked Polly. Ellie went on again.

"Well I had a bit of luck there. One evening as I was driving away to buy some food in the local store I came across one of the trucks which had a puncture and the driver was changing the wheel with his mate. I stopped to ask if I could help and I had my electronic reader in my pocket so I pointed it through the curtain and sure enough the reader picked up the numbers from the things inside the truck. They all came from here".

"Where do you think they're getting all this stuff from?" asked Jake.

Ellie took her iPhone out of her pcket. She attached a small thin cable to the phone and plugged the other end into the USB port on her laptop. Then she showed us a series of images she'd down-loaded from the computers in the cctv room at Cottesloe.

"It took me quite a while to figure out how to hack in to their computers", she said "because I wasn't in the cctv room every evening and I was only there on my own once in a while. I had to work very fast. Anyway, here's what I got".

The first lot of images were lists of items of equipment taken from merchants' delivery notes and insurance brokers' cover notes. This meant that the computer operator had prior knowledge of every item and where it was. "They must have several 'moles' who get the information", said Ellie.

The second image was a Google Earth aerial photograph of each site where equipment had been delivered. This was linked to a GPS reader and the postcode of the delivery point. A MultiMap shot was on the next screen.

Next were lists of all the gangmasters employing migrant labour on farms and market gardens and orchards in each area where Golf GB had a course, and lists of each person working for the gangmaster. There were plenty of people working in the strawberry fields and picking asparagus, soft fruit, top fruit, potatoes and other vegetables and so on who were only too ready to earn themselves a few quid extra by stealing equipment.

On each gangmaster's list there were a few names with asterisks next to them and these were the 'trusties' who could be relied on to carry out night-time operations. "Like the artful dodger and his gang in Oliver Twist", said Ellie.

The next shot was a summary of the police Farm Watch website reports for the past two years. There were numerous items which had been highlighted and these were presumably those which had involved activity by the gangs working for Cottesloe.

There were dozens of screens showing self-billing invoices for golf equipment maintenance. No details, just a bland description: 'Equipment maintenance as requested'. Included in these were the monthly invoices with payment details to Jakellie. There were eight other organisations who carried out the same services as Jakellie throughout the UK. The total billings came to more than a hundred thousand pounds a month.

There were copies of other invoices paid by Cottesloe for concrete drills, plasma cutters, bolt croppers, angle grinders, GPS and satnavs, and other incriminating items.

There were lists of shipping documents and customs declarations and Channel Tunnel fees and road toll charges. All destined for eastern Europe, "probably Russia, that's where all the money is" says Ellie. She switched off her computer and detached her iPhone.

We all looked at each other. It was a huge operation.

"There's no paper trail", said Ellie "everything is electronic. All documents are scanned into the system on arrival and then shredded". Just like Fidelity, I thought, I'd done their audit whilst at KPMG and there was no paper trail.

"A home for retired greyhounds collects the shredded paper once a fortnight, they use it for bedding for the dogs", said Ellie.

We all sat in silence for quite a long time, letting the enormity of the situation sink in. Jake broke into our thoughts.

"This means we've been handling stolen goods", he said, "for quite a time. This was quite innocent when we thought the stuff belonged to Golf GB but now we know it doesn't we can hardly go on with that part of our business. If we decide to close it down now what reason can we give? And besides, what'll happen to all the people who work for us under our apprentice schemes? And what the hell should we do with our knowledge anyway – tell the police I suppose?"

We talked it through for quite a while. We decided it would be best to sleep on it, at least until after the week-end. We also thought it would be a good idea to talk it over with Frank and Kate, after all they were also involved with Pedro Vargas. We agreed to be in touch with Ellie and Jake the following Monday.

Polly and I drove home, each wrapped in our own thoughts. We got ready the following morning to drive up to Cambridge where we were spending the week-end with Simon and Georgina to celebrate Simon's sixtieth birthday. Once again Andy and Tracy had agreed to look after Pinky and Perky.

Chapter 7

1

Cambridge in midsummer, the Backs looking superb with their lawns running down to the Cam, the trees leaning over the river, and the wonderful centuries-old stone buildings which had housed generations of students. Peace and tranquility. England at its best.

There was quite a crowd of people at Simon's birthday party, family of course, and old friends, and a smattering of university colleagues and students too. It was a lunchtime party with champagne and canapes and the garden looked absolutely wonderful.

I spent quite a time chatting to Toby Hartridge. He was now working for the Serious Fraud Office. It didn't surprise me, he'd always had a brilliant forensic mind.

"Money laundering and tax avoidance are the perennial problems", he said "but I've been posted to the identity theft branch. This includes battling against people trying to steal companies' as well as individuals' identities. You'd be amazed at the volume of it".

Toby gave me his card. "Give me a ring sometime when you're coming up to Town, we could have lunch together", then he slipped away to mingle with the crowd. Nice one, I thought , but it'll never happen. Toby had bigger fish than me to fry.

I found Polly talking to a man who had left academia and was heading up a venture capital company in the Cambridge Science Park. His head was shaved and sunburned and he wore a cream coloured linen suit and had a heavy gold medalion hanging on a chain under his jazzy shirt, the top three buttons of which were undone. Polly introduced me.

"As I was saying", he said "we are constantly on the look-out for new businesses to invest in, that's why we're based up here", he paused for a moment, "Britain is one of the most innovative nations in the world, but the problem in Britain is that just as soon as a business reaches a decent size the owners want to cash-in their chips and sell it off. Then it's bought by an overseas company. That's why most of our businesses are owned by foreigners, all of our power generators, motor manufacturers, steel foundaries, electronics, pharmaceuticals", he paused to see if he had our undivided attention, then he went on with the lecture,

"Instead of the 'get rich quick' culture we've adopted from America we should be copying the German and Scandinavian style of businesses – the hidden champions – have you read Hermann Simon's book?" Polly and I both looked at him.

Then he laughed. "But I mustn't get on my hobby horse on a beautiful day like today, how do you fit in here?" he looked at me.

"I'm Georgina's nephew", I said "my father was her brother".

"It's funny to think of Georgie as an aunt" said the venture capitalist "she's lusted after by every don in Cambridge".

"What a great exit line", said Polly as he slipped away to join a group of women standing by the drinks table. What a prick, I thought. But he was right about *Hidden Champions*, I'd read the book several times.

Georgina had invited Polly and me to stay on for supper and to stay the night afterwards.

"It'll give us an opportunity to catch up" she'd said on the phone when I'd rung to say we'd love to come to Simon's birthday party. I'd told her that Polly was expecting a baby. "Oh how wonderful", she'd said, "Bill and Effie would have been so happy".

We had a lovely evening sitting out in the garden in the moonlight till quite late. There were tiny photovoltaic-powered lights stuck into the flower beds and into the borders in the garden and these cast a surreal glow onto the plants growing there.

Simon brought us up to date. He was due to retire at the end of the following academic year but would stay on as Emeritus Profesor of Botany. He was planning to publish a series on all the plants which had been imported into Britain, in conjunction with the RHS and Kew Gardens. It would include biographies of the most famous plant hunters, including Bulley and Forrest and Wilson.

"This'll be published on-line", he said "it'll mean that we can easily add things and keep it up-to-date without the cost of rehashing the text and illustrations or reprinting everything. Besides, the pictures will be much more spectacular on a screen than on paper, and anyone who wants to will be able to print copies for themselves as well. It'll be free of course".

How typically generous of him, I thought. Sharing knowledge and information was much more important to him than money.

"Of course it will mean that Georgina and I will be able to travel a lot more", and he looked across at my aunt and gave her a wink. She grinned at him.

"Time for bed", she said, "sleep well you two" and we all got up slowly and strolled back to the house. Georgina hugged Polly and gave her a kiss.

"You look so well", she said "pregnancy suits you".

I had a terrible nightmare that night. We were sailing in the Solent in a storm. I was at the helm and Polly had been washed overboard by a huge wave and was trapped under *Cinnabar Moth* and the genoa sheet was wrapped around her legs so that she was being dragged along and whatever I tried to do I couldn't raise her up. Her head kept thudding against the hull. I just knew she would drown. When eventually I awoke from the dream I lay there covered in sweat and when I eventually realised that it had only been a dream the relief was so palpable that I started to weep like a child. It took me ages to get back to sleep. I didn't mention the dream to Polly the next morning.

After breakfast Simon suggested that he show me the latest collection of plants which he'd brought back from a recent trip he and Georgina had made to Turkey. We went to his heated greenhouse which was an ancient Victorian structure which had been built against the wall of the garden and which had originally housed a vine and peaches and apricots.

Simon had modernised the interior of the greenhouse but without spoiling the outward design. He showed me the wonderful tulips he'd brought back and some samples of a stunning 'new' orchid too. This reminded me that I'd brought the plant which Frank Waller had given us to show to Simon and I went to the car and got it out of the boot. I handed it to Simon.

"Can you identify this?" I asked him.

Simon took the pot and removed the protective wrapping. He examined the plant carefully, turning it around and feeling the leaves and looking at the stem.

"Where did you get this from?" he asked.

I told him the story which Frank had told me. Simon laughed and then looked serious.

"Do you have any idea what this plant is?"

"Well I thought it might be a tea plant or a camellia, it looked a bit like that family", I replied, "why, what is it?"

"Erythroxylum", said Simon, "the coca plant. Cocaine is extracted from its leaves. It's absolutely forbidden to grow this plant in Europe except under strict licencing regulations and then only for medical research purposes. Strictly speaking you ought to report this to someone at the Home Office. My God, a million and a half plants, they must be worth a king's ransom". I stared at him. He looked back at me.

"Here, why not leave this with me for safe-keeping – as an extra birthday present if you like – and you can have one of my new orchids in exchange. Maybe your friend Frank could propagate some cuttings for me", and he took the Coca plant and put it on one of the slatted shelves in his greenhouse and gave me one of the small orchids.

Driving home to Sussex along the M11 towards London I was very silent.

"Penny for your thoughts", said Polly.

I told her about the coca plant. She was absolutely struck dumb for a few minutes, then she said:

"It's a double whammy for the Waller family. First stolen goods – that's bad enough – but now illegal drug material", and she stopped talking in mid-stream "and I bet I know where all those plants are".

"Where?" I asked.

"Well, I bet they're not in Brazil, I bet they're in those domes in the quarry. They can create a mini-climate in those domes so as to replicate the climate in Brazil or Colombia or wherever they grow the stuff. In fact they would probably grow much faster in the domes than they would in their normal environment. The building that's next to the domes looks just like a laboratory too".

All the way home we discussed the problems of the Waller family. Polly summed it all up just as we were reaching our place.

"It's not our bag, but we're caught up in this thing. We have to support Frank and Effie and Jake. We have to make sure that they do the right thing without us interfering. Most of all we need to be certain that they don't come to any harm. The people they're dealing with will probably stop at nothing to preserve their crooked organisation."

"Well at least they don't know how much we know about them", I said "in that particular we're ahead of them. I think I'll ask Toby Hartridge to run a search on Pedro Vargas, I'll call him in the morning. Then we'll get in touch with the Wallers".

We forgot all about it as soon as we got home, Pinky and Perky gave us a huge welcome and we took them for a long walk all round the paddocks and the garden.

2

I had a meeting the following morning with some potential new clients, but I managed to call Toby on my hands-free cellphone as I was driving to the meeting. He said he would get on to Pedro Vargas straight away and asked me for my email address. He sounded very friendly and seemed glad I had called him.

My meeting was with a group of dairy farmers who were members of a costings group run by a consultant called Rex. There were about twenty-five members in the group and the consultant visited each of them once a month and checked their performance by margin per cow and per acre. He published a league table with a code number for each herd but of course all the farmers knew who was who in the list. The group had been going for a long time and each farmer valued their membership highly.

There was a lot more to the group than just the bare financial results. They got a lot of feedback, including bought feed analysis, veterinary advice, dissemination of new ideas and methods and they benefitted from the knowledge that they were all in the same boat so that when they thought things were going well or badly they could see each month that all the others were doing about the same. Every now and then they visited research establishments or farms as a group and this formed a strong bond between them all.

I had been recommended by my animal psychologist client who had been told by Rex that the accountant who looked after the members of his dairy group had decided to retire and they were looking for a replacement. Now I was going to be grilled by all these guys.

When I entered the upper room where the meeting was being held in The Swan Inn at Petworth, I noticed an overpowering smell of chemicals which I later discovered was the material which they used for the circulation cleaning of their milking plants. This not only cleaned and disinfected the bulk tank and the milk line and all the mlking clusters but removed any milkstone as well, so it was pretty powerful stuff. You certainly didn't have to ask what they did for a living. I was asked to sit at the end of the table and then Rex poured me a coffee and turned to me.

"Tom, these people represent the bulk of my clients. Those who aren't here have told me they'll go along with whatever is decided today. They want you to tell them why you think you should take over as their accountant".

I sipped my coffee and looked around the table. Sixteen faces including two women. It was quite daunting really. I sipped my coffee again. I felt glad I had decided never to wear a suit. It would have looked completely out of place in this company.

"Well," I said "I can obviously prepare your accounts and agree your tax with the Revenue. I can do this for a fixed fee based on the size of your herd, provided you can supply me with accurate up-to-date figures and all the necessary vouchers to go with them". I paused and looked around the table again. Then I went on.

"I can also advise you on various more interesting things. These could include preparing budgets for bank loans if you decide to expand your business or to diversify. It could include advice on how to prepare for retirement, and arranging for succession if you have a relative to take over the farm. It could include advice on growing your pension fund with off-farm investments, including a cottage or a house for you to live in. I can do this and anything else you ask me to. I would discuss it with you and agree a fixed fee in advance so that you knew what you were up for".

I went on again "I would also let Rex have regular bulletins of technical data which might be useful for some or all of you to know about and which Rex could bring round with him during each visit. These would be very short, just highlighting new legislation or ideas but enough for you to decide if you wanted to take it any further".

I stopped talking and grinned at Rex. "That's about it", I said "you can let me know what they decide", and I stood up to leave.

"Not so fast", said one of the older farmers, "as far as I'm concerened you tick all the boxes and I'm sure everyone else here will agree. Let us take you out to lunch if you've the time".

Suddenly the room seemed to come alive and everyone started talking at once, and I was surrounded by a group of eager, friendly people all of whom seemed to agree that I ticked their boxes as well. It was a marvellous feeling and I suddenly relaxed. Wow, I thought, twenty-five new clients in one go. I must ring my animal psychologist client and thank him very much for the introduction. I couldn't wait to tell Polly as well.

Driving back to the office after sandwiches and more coffee I counted up the new clients I'd taken on during the past couple of months. There was an importer of welding machines, a couple of restaurants, a wholesale dealer in industrial chemicals, a firm of solicitors and an estate agent. And now twenty-five dairy farmers. Polly and I would have to set up some pretty neat processes to be able to cope with the expansion.

When I got back to the office I found an email from Toby in my inbox.

Pedro Vargas. Brazilian subject. Born Salvador, Bahia. Married (1) Catarina da Silva. 2 sons 3 daughters. Large estates in Bahia (approx 112,000 Ha). Investments in ethanol, beef, coffee, cement, oil. Multi-millionaire, maybe even billionaire. Wife died. Moved operations and home to UK. Married (2) Jennifer de Candole. 1 son 1 daughter. Owner/founder of Golf GB and Paradigm Hotels. Houses in Sussex, London and Monte Carlo. Founder Brazilian Rainforest Conservation charity. Roving ambassador for UNICEF. Wife involved with Save the Children. Owner of Brazilian America's Cup challenger 'Condor'. Just taken delivery of a new Benetti luxury 85m yacht 'Tabebuia Alba' built especially for PV in Italy. Member Royal Yacht Squadron at Cowes IOW. Will be hosting Brazilian Olympic sailing team and other dignatories on board Tabebuia Alba during Cowes week.

I read the email through a couple of times and acknowledged it with thanks to Toby. Then I sat and thought about it for a while.

I came to the conclusion that it begged more questions than it answered. Why did Pedro come to the UK? Does he still own all his Brazilian assets? Does he know what's going on at Cottesloe and in the quarry – both the 'recycling' business and the cocaine? Besides, what exactly is going on in the laboratory-style building and in the domes in the quarry?

Then I thought about our own position. Should we get involved anyway, after all it isn't our business? The whole situation posed a series of conundrums. Why not just walk away from the whole thing and let it all happen and get on with our own lives? Besides, Polly and I will soon be parents with added responsibilities.

I knew what Polly would say.

"Rubbish", she'd say "they're friends and clients of ours - we have to help them as much as we can", and she'd be right of course. But we were getting out of our depth and out of our comfort zone, to mix two metaphors.

I forwarded the Pedro Vargas biography to Frank and to Ellie with no comment. And I heard nothing back from them. Things just went quiet.

3

I got an urgent call from Fred Clements, one of my new clients whose business was a chemical wholesaler called Chemco Solutions. He needed help completing his VAT return because there had been quite a number of transactions with European companies and he wasn't sure how to deal with them in the return. It was a good opportunity to take a closer look at the business anyway. Fred had got a degree in Chemistry at London University and I guessed he must be pretty smart.

Chemco's business was split into two parts. First it sold chemicals direct to large organisations like swimming pool suppliers, laundries and agricultural merchants. These sales were bulk orders for large amounts of product. The second part of the business was sales of items which Chemco repackaged in smaller amounts and sold to shops and organisations which sold the products over the counter to end-users.

While I was checking the transactions for the quarter I turned up a cash invoice for large quantities of baking soda, inositol and citric acid. Really huge amounts, costing several thousand pounds. A bell rang in my head.

"Big transactions and funny transactions" the lecturer had said at the CPE lecture on auditing. This transaction was both big and funny. I asked Fred Clements about the sale.

"That's the third order we've had from that customer in the last few months", said Fred. "Each time we get a phone call giving us a couple of days to get the stuff together. No name on the invoice, just a cash invoice. Always pays cash. An unmarked white van turns up to collect the boxes, a bloke in overalls picks it all up, pays cash and off he goes. We could do with more customers like that!"

"What's the stuff for?" I asked.

"Ask no questions...." said Fred "....and you'll be told no lies". Then he looked serious.

"Actually I'm quite worried about it. You see these substances, which are harmless in themselves are used mainly in food production but they're also used as cocaine adulterants, in other words they're substances which are 'cut' with cocaine to dilute it and the dealer makes a lot more money as a result".

"And you've no idea where the stuff goes to?" I asked.

"No" replied Fred, "but last time I wrote down the registration number of the white Ford Transit van". He looked in his diary. "Here it is: LZ 07 PGG".

I didn't say anything but I made a mental note of the number and then I changed the subject to gross and net profits and we dicussed whether it would be better for Fred to pay himself a bonus or a dividend out of this year's profits.

When I got home that evening I suggested to Polly that we should take Pinky and Perky for their walk after supper on Cottesloe Golf Course. I wanted to take another look at the quarry.

We took our binoculars with us as we always did for bird-watching. When we reached the fence between the golf course and the quarry we found that the hole which the dogs had got through the previous time had been repaired with heavy-duty weld mesh and was completely wired up.

"There's a place along the bank where we can look down into the quarry from this side of the fence", said Polly, so we inched our way along the outside of the fence until we reached the spot. It was almost dark by now.

We looked down into the quarry through our binoculars. We could see everything very clearly in the floodlights. It was all quiet on the western front.

"Look, there's a white Transit van", said Polly and sure enough there it was parked in the lee of the building which Polly always referred to as the lab. We could read the registration number quite clearly. LZ 07 PGG.

"That's the baby", I said.

"We just have to find out what on earth's going on in this quarry", said Polly.

"We'll call the Wallers in the morning and arrange another meeting", I said. And so we did.

But the Wallers seemed reluctant to talk about anything to do with Pedro Vargas or Cottesloe or stolen equipment or coca plants or even white vans, in fact they didn't want to talk about anything at all. They said they were too busy with other stuff even to make a date for a meeting.

"Leave them be", said Polly "they'll get in touch if they want anything.

4

I spent the next morning at home with Polly working on an idea I'd had for designing a template for the accounts of similar businesses. With the dairy group I could now put this into practice. Polly made a few suggestions and I decided to go ahead with it.

About mid-morning I got a text from Jake.

Ellie missing believe kidnapped please meet fountain inn ashurst 7 tonight jake

"When troubles come they come not single file but in battalions", said Polly. "You'd best go alone to meet Jake, he doesn't need a crowd. Be very careful though".

I decided to spend the rest of the day catching up with routine stuff, the sort of things which had to be done but could pretty well be achieved on automatic pilot, so as to fill the time until I had to leave for my meeting with Jake. I had a bad premonition about this business, it might suddenly get ugly. Could the text message be a trap? Get a grip, I told myself.

I decided to arrive at The Fountain a bit after seven o'clock. It was another lovely summer evening and the verges on the sides of the road were filled with cow parsley and milkweed and some wild poppies. The foxgloves were starting to grow tall too.

I parked up outside the primary school which is next to The Fountain and walked round to the back of the pub to look through the window. Jake was sitting on his own at a corner table. The bar was almost empty except for the usual locals. I went through the rear door into the bar as if I'd just come out of the WC and walked over and sat at Jake's table.

"What would you like to drink?" asked Jake.

"Just an orange juice and lemonade please", I replied. Better keep my wits about me, I thought. Jake came back to the table with a couple of glasses.

"How's Polly?" he asked.

"Fine thanks", I replied "she's getting quite large now with the baby".

"Shall we sit outside?" said Jake, "it's such a lovely evening", and without waiting for an answer he led the way to a table on the pub lawn as far away as possible from the bar.

"Why did you want to meet here?" I asked Jake.

"Because it's where I often eat my evening meal when I'm on my own and it won't arouse any suspicion if I'm seen. I'm just part of the furniture.", he answered.

"Tell me about Ellie", I said.

Jake leant forward, looked at me, blinked a couple of times and said

"Ellie's been disappearing for a few days at a time on a regular basis ever since we last met. She just won't leave it alone. She's become paranoid about Cottesloe". He sipped his drink.

"I've got a friend called Brigid Fortune who works at the Wildfowl and Wetland Trust place at Arundel, in fact I've often helped her with projects she's involved with because I'm really interested in bird migration and quite worried about the reduction in the numbers of species of birds over the past few years".

I got the impression that Jake might also be really interested in Brigid but I didn't say so.

"Anyway", said Jake "I'd been helping Brigid to fasten some electronic trackers on to swans' legs so that the WWT can get real live information about the details of their migration. These latest gadgets are very sophisticated and give out signals so that you can track their flights to their wintering places and when the birds come back again to breed next season you can take off the trackers and download all the information onto a laptop. It tells you how much time the bird has been in the air or on water or land and through a GPS system exactly where". He paused again and took another sip of his drink.

"Well I asked Brigid if she could lend or give me a couple of the old-type trackers which the WWT wasn't using any more which merely plotted the GPS position of the wearer at any time and which could be read by anyone who logged on to the correct wavelength with a mobile phone or a laptop. She went and found two of the old trackers and gave them to me". He looked at me.

"When I got home that evening I attached one of the trackers to Ellie's car and I fitted the other into a pendant she always wears round her neck which contains a lock of our mother's hair and which I know she never opens. The trackers are roughly the size of a mobile phone sim card. Of course I didn't tell Ellie what I'd done".

"Over the next few days I followed Ellie's movements. I felt really guilty about it but I just felt it was essential for her safety that someone knew where she was. She's got a new cleaning job working as personal assistant to the owner of the agency who cleans out the 'lab' at the quarry. It's a very high security job and only trusties are allowed to do it".

"Two nights ago Ellie's boss had to go home early because one of her kids was ill and she left Ellie on her own in the quarry to finish off the work. This was too good an opportunity to miss and Ellie started to explore the lab and eventually the domes, I could see her movements on my screen".

"The first indication I had that all was not well was that her personal tracker showed that she was travelling quite fast in a vehicle whilst the tracker on her car remained stationary in the car park. She was in someone else's vehicle. Over the next couple of hours the vehicle drove all the way to Potsmouth, then it went across to Cowes on the ferry and finally parked by the seafront. The tracker showed Ellie travelling a short distance along the front and then across the water for another short distance and then remaining stationary on the water. I worked out that Ellie was on a boat of some kind".

"This was yesterday" said Jake "and I've been worried to death about her ever since. She doesn't answer her mobile. Frank and Kate are away and I didn't know who else to turn to, so I texted you".

"Come back to our place" I said "and we can think of a plan with Polly".

5

When we got home Polly cooked us some bacon and eggs and we sat round the kitchen table with mugs of scalding, strong tea. Jake spent some time cleaning his spectacles and then immediately blowing on the lenses and going through the same palaver all over again. He's in a terrible state of nerves, I thought.

"Now I've been thinking", said Polly. We both looked at her. "I think the best plan is for you two to go down to Hayling Island and sail *Cinnabar Moth* over to Cowes. There are several advantages to this. You'll arrive by boat which no-one will expect. Let's face it they –

whoever they are – will be on the lookout for Ellie's people to do something and they'll be checking every ferry which docks on the island. Also you'll be able to live on board which will be a great advantage, you can use it as your base while you're looking for Ellie, and finally when you've found Ellie you'll be able to sail back with her".

Jake seemed quite positive about this plan. The inaction and uncertainty were killing him. We made a list of everything we'd need for the adventure, including water, provisions, fuel, torches and batteries, clothing and towels and sleeping bags.

"Remember to charge the boat's battery as soon as you get to the marina", said Polly "you'll need to have it fully charged if you're live on board. You'll need to be able to charge your laptop and cellphone batteries and it'll mean the boat's battery will be getting a lot of usage". I wrote this on the list too.

"Shall we sleep here tonight?" I asked Jake "then we can make an early start and drive down to Hayling via your place so's you can pick up the things you'll need". Jake nodded. Polly showed him up to the little spare room which we'd converted from a loft space in the roof of the house.

I kissed Polly goodbye and Jake and I drove in tandem to Jake's house at about five o'clock the following morning He left his car parked outside the garage so that anyone passing the gate could see it and would assume that he was at home. Then he gathered all his stuff and put it in a soft zip-up bag and set the intruder alarm and locked the door as we left. I drove down the familiar route towards the Chichester bypass. Jake spent most of the time fiddling with his Blackberry and polishing his spectacles. There was no change in the signals from either of Ellie's trackers.

We stopped at the Sainsbury's at the roundabout which leads into Chichester and bought all the things on our list. Then we drove on round the bypass to the Hayling Island turn-off and stopped at the chandlers to get the bits and pieces we needed for the boat. We parked up in the members' car park at the marina and by degrees got all our things on board *Cinnabar Moth*. I remembered to plug the cable from the electricity supply at the marina into our battery so as to charge it up before we left. When we got on board I was quite surprised to find that Jake was pretty handy in the boat, and I said as much.

"I've done quite a bit of sailing with Brigid actually", he said "she's got an old Folkboat which used to belong to her father. We go out in it quite often together". Then he blushed and started the old spectacle polishing lark again. A dark horse, I thought to myself.

We got everything stowed and checked the level in the gas bottle, topped up the fuel tank for the engine and checked the oil, checked the level of the water in the bilges and pumped them out, and found the chart for the Solent. Then we got out the genoa and slid the battens into the mainsail ready to hoist it when we got outside the harbour. We made a couple of mugs of tea and ate some digestive biscuits with them.

"My Blackberry has a GPS app on it", said Jake "so I'll set it up for this area", and he spent a few minutes concentrating on doing this.

"Set to go?" I said, and Jake nodded.

We unplugged the electric supply cable, started the engine, cast off the dock lines and motored slowly out into the harbour channel and on towards the Winner sandbank and out into the sea. We hoisted the main and the genoa and adjusted the sheets. There was a nice breeze from the south-west and I thought what fun it would be to be sailing with Polly and not embarking on this madcap venture.

I thought privately to myself that it would have been much better to have put the whole thing into the hands of the police, then I thought of Ellie and how she might be in danger, almost certainly was in danger, and my blood ran cold and I tried not to think of it and concentrated instead on keeping Cinnabar Moth tramping along in the breeze which by now had stiffened to about force four as we sailed out of the shadow of the mainland.

We sailed on past Spitbank Fort and into the east Solent. Jake seemed to have assumed the role of navigator and was busy with the chart and his GPS and a pencil and was laying a course from Spitbank to Cowes. We passed a few yachts out practising for Cowes Week which was due to start in a few days' time, and saw a number of ferries and tankers. We eventually reached Cowes and found a swinging mooring in Cowes Roads where we tied up.

"This wouldn't have been available next week", I said, as we stowed the genoa in its sail bag, tied the mainsail to the boom and sorted out the sheets and clipped the halyards to the mast fittings, "there'll be literally hundreds of yachts trying to find a mooring".

Jake didn't say anything in reply. He had his Blackberry out and was seated in the cockpit pointing it towards the Squadron. It bleeped several times.

"That's where Ellie is", he said and pointed towards an enormous vessel which was anchored just off the Squadron lawn. Jake got out his binoculars and screwed the eyepiece slowly round until the vessel came into focus. He read out the name on the stern.

"*Tabebuia Alba*", he said.

"Pedro Vargas", we both cried in unison. We sat side-by-side in the cockpit and discussed what we should do.

"Ultimately we need to get on board and find Ellie", I said "but we can't just rock up as bold as brass and expect to get away with it. These guys have a lot at stake. Hayling Yacht Club has reciprocal rights with The Island Sailing Club, so let's walk along and have a drink and get a closer look at *Tabebuia Alba*".

I signed on Jake in the visitors' book at the entrance to the club and we went up the staircase, past the famous photograph of *Susanne* under full sail, and into the bar. It always gave me a thrill to see Beken's famous photograph, *Susanne* had seventeen sails set and filled with wind. There was a notice behind the bar advertising a function on board *Tabebuia Alba* on the

145

evening of the following day to welcome the Brazilian olympic sailing team which was in Britain to practice for the olympics. Tickets at £75 per person were available at the bar, all proceeds to Save the Children. Dinner and dancing till midnight. Black tie.

We sat in the window and had a pot of coffee and some tuna and mayonnaise sandwiches.

"That's the way to get on board without any fuss", I said "go to the dinner/dance".

"We'd need partners", said Jake defensively.

"Then I'll call Polly and get her to arrange to bring Brigid down in the car with our dinner jackets and all the kit and kaboodle. We'll find a couple of rooms in a bed and breakfast place where we can put up for a couple of nights and change into our things. What's Brigid's number?"

I could see that Jake wasn't used to making these sorts of decisions. He was more of a backroom boy or techie and he obviously hated any kind of confrontation. He'd always depended on his elder brother and sister to drive things on and he'd been happy to follow them. Now, because of Ellie's predicament and the fact that Frank wasn't around he was being forced to make up his mind for himself. Out came the handkerchief and he rubbed the lenses of his spectacles and blinked at me. I suddenly realised that there could be another angle to his worries. He would have to share a room with Brigid with all that this might entail.

I waited for him to reply and I looked out of the window at the tranquil scene outside. Cowes in midsummer. Serene, reliable, unique. Then I looked left at *Tabebuia Alba* and I wondered what was happening on board. Jake was fiddling with his Blackberry.

My cellphone bleeped. I opened the message.

Business Card: Brigid Fortune +7776543897.

Jake had made his decision. I glanced at him and saw he too was looking at *Tabebuia Alba*. Poor old Jake, he must be in a turmoil.

"I'll go and call Polly", I said. "Have some more coffee and then when I get back we'll go and find a B and B where we can stay. OK?" He nodded his agreement.

6

When I got back to the club after arranging everything with Polly, Jake was looking much happier. I sat down and was about to tell him what Polly and I had arranged when he thrust a copy of Yachting World at me. I looked at the feature on the page which was open: YACHT OF THE MONTH. Jake's eyes were shining with excitement.

It was the May issue and I saw that the yacht of the month was *Tabebuia Alba* with a fourteen page article all about her, including plans of the yacht itself with the layout of each deck, specifications of the two massive Deutz diesel engines, the navigation equipment, and photographs of the interior of the vessel, and details of the naval architects and Benetti the boat builders in

Italy. She was hailed as the finest motor yacht to have been built this century, even better than Roman Abramovitch's yacht *Eclipse*.

"That'll be useful", I said "well spotted. We'll borrow the magazine for a day or two, it'll make our job easier when we get on board *Tabebuia Alba.* By the way Polly just texted me to say that she and Brigid will be catching the six o'clock ferry this evening so we'd better get our skates on and find some lodgings".

I went up to the bar and bought four tickets for the function on *Tabebuia Alba* the following evening. Then we strolled out of the club. I had the Yachting World tucked under my arm.

At our third attempt we were lucky to find two double rooms in a boarding house a few streets back from the front. The landlady told us that she had just had two cancellations. The rooms were comfortable with en-suite bathrooms. They didn't do an evening meal, just breakfast.

"Shall we book a table for four for supper at Murrays Seafood Restaurant", I suggested to Jake and he confirmed that Brigid and he both liked fish.

We had a few hours to kill before the ferry was due so we decided to go for a walk into the countryside south of the town. It was a fine day, but windy and we had a good blow.

Jake had become much more positive with the thought of a plan of action and as a result he was more talkative than usual. He told me that he'd like to be an inventor and when I asked him what sort of things he would like to invent he answered that he wasn't really sure but maybe it would be fun to invent things to help handicapped people to be more mobile.

"We don't do nearly enough to make their lives more normal", said Jake "the goal should be to try and make everything just as accessible for them as it is for us. The last thing they want is for people to feel sorry for them, they want to be treated like everyone else, and the best way to achieve this would be to give them an opportunity to do everything we can do".

His face was glowing with the effort of walking briskly up the hill and with his enthusiasm for what was obviously a real passion. I suddenly felt I knew him much better and I admired his attitude. We had a healthy walk and then went back to *Cinnabar Moth* to collect our things and move into our rooms at the boarding house. Then we went down to the ferry terminal to meet Polly and Brigid when they docked.

Chapter 8

1

After enjoying a fish supper of moules marinières with a glass of Pinot Grigio at Murray's the four of us went for a walk along the front. Brigid had turned out to be a very switched-on person, attractive and amusing and also very obviously fond of Jake. They lingered further and further behind Polly and me as we walked along so that in the end we lost touch with them and we eventually ended up just the two of us having a coffee in a bar looking across the Solent to Southampton Water on the mainland. If it hadn't been for the worrying reason for our being there it would have seemed just like a holiday.

As we sat watching the sun go down and saw the last of the birds flying to their roosts in the trees and bushes and buildings around us, Polly suddenly looked serious and leant towards me so that no-one could have heard what she said.

"Tomorrow might be quite dangerous", she murmured "this guy Vargas has so much at stake he can't afford to be thwarted by a bunch of amateurs like us".

She paused to let her words sink in.

"I've been thinking. Nobody knows we're here or that Ellie is almost certainly being held captive on board *Tabebuia Alba* . We ought to let someone know what's going on. Someone independent and absolutely reliable".

"Have you got anyone in mind?" I asked her.

"Well, what about Toby Hartridge?", she replied. "He's rock solid and besides, he's working for a government department which is involved with crime — especially fraud. He's your cousin and you know him as well as anybody. I think you should either email or text him with a brief summary of where we are and what we're doing and the circumstances surrounding Ellie's disappearance. At least then we'll have cover if anything goes wrong".

I suddenly felt a chill in the night air and a shiver ran down my spine. Dangerous, she'd said. A bunch of amateurs. And Polly pregnant and vulnerable. It was a hideous prospect and I didn't want to think about it.

"I haven't got my laptop", I said, cursing myself for the oversight.

"No, but I have", said Polly, "I brought it down in my overnight case, so it's in our room. You can plan what you're going to say to Toby and compose an email and send it to him tomorrow before breakfast".

As usual Polly was absolutely right.

"OK", I said, "I'll do just that". I realised what a good idea it was, and immediately felt more relaxed. We strolled back to our room and went to bed. There was no sign of the other two but their key wasn't on the numbered hook behind the desk so we guessed they must have gone to bed too.

I had another dreadful nightmare that night. Again we were fighting huge waves on board *Cinnabar Moth*, this time somewhere out in the Atlantic. Polly was trapped in the fo'c's'le where she'd gone to fetch another sail because the one we were flying had been torn to shreds in the gale. The toggle on the sailbag had caught on a handle which jutted out from the hatch on the foredeck and Polly was unable to climb out. Water from the huge seas was washing over the bow and pouring into the open hatch and I could hear Polly choking on the seawater and fighting for breath. I daren't leave the tiller because the yacht would broach to and we should then be broadside on to the waves and could founder and never be able to bring her head round. I started to panic when I heard Polly shouting for help.

I woke again in a sweat and shaking in every limb as if I had a fever. Eventually I realised that it had only been a dream and I slowly calmed down, but the dread of losing Polly stayed with me for ages and I felt close to tears again.

If this sort of dream were to keep on happening I should soon be afraid to go to sleep, I thought. Eventually I decided to get up and I went into the bathroom and dried myself off with a towel. Then I got hold of my laptop and perched on the edge of the bath with the laptop on my knees and drafted an email to Toby.

I told him all about Ellie and the electronic tags and how we'd sailed over to Cowes and about *Tabebuia Alba* and what we planned to do. He knew about

Vargas anyway. I gave him all of our mobile phone numbers and explained where *Cinnabar Moth* was moored and the address of our boarding house. I saved the email as a draft and went back to bed whereupon I fell into a dreamless sleep and was woken by Polly.

"Get up lazybones", she said "you've got to write your email to Toby". Then she vanished into the bathroom to have a shower. I didn't mention my nightmare or the fact that I'd been up in the night so she was quite surprised when I showed her the draft email later, she thought I must have written it very quickly when she'd been in the shower. Ah well, you've got to get up early to catch a Hardy, I thought.

We all met up in the dining room and had a full English breakfast. Jake and Brigid seemed very relaxed together. After a while Brigid spoke up.

"Presumably there's no point in hanging around here until this evening?" she said, and when we all agreed she went on "because I've always wanted to visit Osborne House but I've never been to the Isle of Wight before, so I thought we might all go and have a look around. The gardens are supposed to be spectacular as well".

"It's very close", said Jake "so it wouldn't take very long to get there. We can go by bus."

"Let's take a picnic and we can eat it in the garden", said Brigid.

We went back to our rooms to get ready for the trip and after making a couple of changes which Polly had suggested, I sent off the email to Toby. Then we locked everything up and met Jake and Brigid downstairs. The landlady had made up some sandwiches for us and Jake put them in his knapsack with his and Brigid's binoculars and an ordnance survey map and four bottles of water.

We had a specially nice day at Osborne, the weather was very kind to us and we walked for miles around the spacious gardens and ate our picnic under a spreading chestnut tree. We then looked around the house and were pleasantly surprised at how small and intimate the rooms were, quite different to the other royal palaces we had been to in the past.

I especially liked the L-shaped drawing room with the billiard table close enough for Albert and his pals to play on and still enjoy contact with his family. From all accounts Albert was a pretty good consort and he and Victoria were happy together, what a shock it must have been to her when Albert suddenly died aged only forty-two. The official cause of death was typhoid, but Albert had been suffering for several years from stomach pains and he most probably died from renal failure or stomach cancer. We shall never know, but what is certain is that the royal marriage was very happy and fruitful.

We very much enjoyed our tour round Osborne and after a cup of tea in the cafetaria we caught the bus back to Cowes to get ready for the function on board *Tabebuia Alba* .

When we got back to our room I found a two word acknowledgement of my email to Toby.

"Roger. Noted." was all it said. He must be very busy and preoccupied, I thought.

2

We arrived at the gangplank to go aboard *Tabebuia Alba* about half an hour after the reception began so as not to be conspicuous. Jake and I had poured over the plans of the vessel in Yachting Monthly so that we knew the layout like the backs of our hands. We had even tested each other on things like the route we would take to go from the bridge to the galley or from the dining room to the owner's suite or where the engine room was in relation to the liferafts. Jake had insisted that we should be as conversant with *Tabebuia Alba* as possible without having actually been on board.

We handed our tickets to a charming couple of stewards and were directed to the after deck where the reception was being held with champagne on arrival. We would then be free to wander around and look at the yacht until dinner which was due to start at eight o'clock. There were to be some short speeches during dinner to introduce the members of the Brazilian Olympic yachting team and Pedro Vargas was to introduce a surprise celebrity who would auction some promises, the proceeds of which were to go to Save the Children. Signora Vargas's favourite charity, I remembered. Dancing would go on until eleven thirty when there would be a firework display from the Squadron lawn.

We strolled around with our glasses of champagne and spent some time looking over the rail at the lights on shore and across to Southampton Water to the north. Eventually we reached the staircase leading down to the cabins and we descended these and found ourselves in a wide corridor with cabin doors on either side. Jake took out his Blackberry and tuned it on to Ellie's frequency. The signal was instant and high.

"She's in one of these cabins aft" said Jake and hurried on towards the rear of *Tabebuia Alba*. We opened the door of one cabin, then another, then a third, but they were all empty. We reached the last door and Jake was just about to grab the handle when the door was opened from inside and Pedro Vargas stood in the doorway. There were a couple of tough-looking minders right behind him, they looked just like Tweedledum and Tweedledee, except that there was nothing humorous about them. Pedro stepped back and the minders came out and stood on either side of us.

"Ah", said Pedro, "we were expecting you, do come in and join your friend", and he stepped aside to allow us to enter a large cabin. Ellie was tied to a chair and she had a gag in her mouth. Jake went as if to go to her but Tweedledum held Jake's arm to prevent him.

"Undo the young lady please", said Pedro to Tweedledee and in a jiffy Ellie was released and the gag was out of her mouth. She stood up and took a few steps and almost fell into Jake's arms.

"Very touching", said Pedro, half smiling. Then his expression changed and he frowned and looked very serious and rather threatening.

"Now", he went on "we've got you all. I can't tolerate any more of your snooping into my affairs. As soon as the party's over at midnight and the fireworks are finished, we're going to up-anchor and head for the Mediterranean. As we pass through the Bay of Biscay we'll be able to feed the fishes" and he leered at each of us in turn.

It was all rather melodramatic. I was suddenly reminded of Vladimir Zukhov sitting in the dock at the Old Bailey. Two of a kind, I thought.

"Now, we'll lock you in here and there'll be a guard outside the door at all times. As you've paid for your dinners I'll make sure you are fed. Please hand over any watches or mobile phones to these two men, I have to go and greet my guests", and so saying he left us.

Tweedledum and Tweedledee did a thorough job of searching us and took all our mobiles and watches and pens and credit cards and cash as well. They left with the swag, looking smug and self-satisfied.

As soon as we were satisfied that Ellie was alright we made a throrough search of the cabin. It was a luxurious suite with a double bedroom with an ensuite bathroom, a smaller bedroom with twin beds, a separate bathroom and a small annexe with a television and writing table with provision for a computer – but there was no computer there. We felt rather flat and all sat down in the main cabin to think things over, and we asked Ellie to tell us what she had found in the quarry and how she had come to be caught and abducted.

As it happened Ellie had actually discovered very little at the quarry. She couldn't get into any part of the laboratory except for the office and kitchen and toilets, no outside cleaners ever went into the laboratory itself or into the store rooms or refrigerated zones. As for the domes, they were also impossible to get into and were filled with a dense fog or mist so that Ellie could only vaguely see the plants inside, although she said it looked like a positive jungle of vegetation.

Ellie had been about to leave after finishing her shift in the laboratory office when two men had turned up wearing overalls and knocked on the door and she had let them in thinking that they had forgotten their keys.

"That's her", said one of the men and the other had grabbed Ellie and they had rolled her up in a rug and carried her outside and put her in the back of a transit van. They had actually treated her quite gently and she was unharmed although very scared.

There followed an interminable journey in the back of the van, it was very uncomfortable lying on the ridged metal floor, and several times she had rolled across from one side to the other as they had gone round corners. After what seemed like an age they had reached a place where she could hear the sea and sure enough she heard the wheels of the transit running on hollow-sounding timber as they went on board the ferry.

She heard the loudspeaker informing passengers that they would be leaving in five minutes for the Isle of Wight so that then she knew where they were bound for. Later she had been carried on board and they had put her in this cabin and fed her and made sure she was comfortable. It was only when the party had begun that she was tied to the chair and gagged so as to make sure that she couldn't scream or try to escape. Then we had arrived.

At this point she lost it and burst into tears and Brigid and Jake had to console and comfort her until she recovered. We all sat silently for a while with our own thoughts. I cursed myself for allowing Polly to get involved in this escapade, I should have known better. What was I thinking? We must have been out of our minds to even contemplate taking Vargas on, with all his wealth and influence we were no match for him. Now I was going to live – or die – to rue the day. I felt absolutely desperate.

3

Judging from the noise and laughter the dinner party was a great success. We heard the speeches but only very faintly, and we knew when each speech had ended because there was applause followed by chords of music from the band. It must have been someone's birthday because they played 'Happy birthday to you' and this was followed by more laughter and clapping. Then the band struck up and the dancing began.

It was a lovely moonlit night and we could see the occasional lights of ships going westward out of the

Solent down channel through the windows. It was noticeable that the cabin had large windows instead of the old-fashioned portholes of earlier yachts. I thought if only we were on holiday instead of being trapped as prisoners what fun it would be, but trapped we were, with no escape.

Suddenly we heard the key turn in the lock and Tweedledum appeared in the threshold.

"Your dinners" he announced, and two stewards came through the door dressed smartly in the *Tabebuia Alba* livery, each pushing a large trolley. Tweedledum went back outside and locked the door again, evidently to avoid any chance of us trying to escape or to rush him.

One of the stewards set up five places on the dining table with cutlery and glasses and serviettes and asked us to be seated. Then he served dinner. It seemed absolutely surreal sitting there watching him dish out our food when we ourselves were prisoners waiting to be 'fed to the fishes' as Pedro Vargas had so eloquently put it. Nevertheless the human spirit is very resilient and we all seemed to be willing to carry on with the charade, besides we were hungry so we started to tuck-in. I remember we ate coronation chicken and salad washed down with chilled sauvignon blanc, and it tasted very good indeed.

The first steward knocked on the door with a pre-arranged signal and Tweedledum opened it for him to push his trolley through and leave the cabin, the door was locked behind him. The second steward waited for a few minutes and then came over to our table. He motioned us to be very quiet and not to say anything. Then he took off his chef's hat and removed a false moustache and stood upright. He was very tall. It was Alex Frenkel. Polly and I were astonished and were just about to exclaim something when again he urgently motioned to us to remain silent.

Then he removed the cloth from the trolley and took five gas masks and five orange flak jackets from inside the containers which would normally have held the desserts. He told us in low tones that we should each put on a gas mask and a flak jacket when we heard the first firework let off. Under no circumstances should we take off the gas masks or the flak jackets until we were off the vessel. Nor should we try to leave the cabin until we were fetched.

Then Alex put the moustache and chef's hat back on and covered the trolley with the cloth and knocked on the door. This time it was Tweedledee who opened it and let the steward out of the cabin and immediately slammed the door shut and locked it. He was evidently much more nervous than Tweedledum.

We waited tensely for the first firework to be let off. It seemed an age. I remembered all the old clichés about time standing still. Then the music stopped and we imagined all the guests trooping off the boat onto the Squadron lawn to watch the display.

Suddenly we heard the first firework — a rocket — whooshing up into the sky and exploding loudly. The moment this happened we put on our gas masks and made sure they fitted tightly. They were labelled S100 gas mask/respirators designed for British and NATO forces. Then we put on our flak jackets. We checked each other to make sure they looked secure. Almost immediately the cabin started to fill with a violet-coloured smoke which was being pumped through the air-conditioning system of the yacht. It seemed it was a form of teargas.

We heard the key in the lock and the door swung open. Tweedledee stood in the doorway gasping for air and swaying with a dreadful look on his face. He stared in disbelief at our gas masks and flak jackets and made as if to come into the cabin and grab one, then he crashed forward on his face and lay inert on the cabin floor. We stayed where we were, remembering Alex's command to remain in the cabin until we were fetched.

After a short time a couple of men in camouflage uniforms and wearing gas masks arrived at the door and stepping over Tweedledee they helped each of us out of the door and the one in front motioned us to follow him while the other brought up the rear. I noticed that they both carried short-barrelled guns.

As we reached the gangplank a posse of police in riot gear boarded the vessel in the opposite direction. We ran at top speed across the Squadron lawn past the disbelieving faces of the guests who had been marshalled to the edge of the lawn by about twenty riot police. The Royal Yacht Squadron had been taken over by the police and the camouflaged forces and we were ushered into the committee room which had been turned into an operations headquarters.

Standing inside the door was Toby Hartridge. He grinned slyly at me.

"Welcome to my world", he said and put his arm around my shoulders. Then he hugged and kissed Polly. "Introduce me to your friends", he said "and we'll have some refreshments".

We introduced Ellie and Jake and Brigid to Toby. Alex came into the room and he too was introduced by Toby.

"Alex is working at the Home Office", said Toby "he's part of the drugs squad. We got to know each other at your housewarming party and we've been friends ever since".

Then we sat round a table in the corner of the room and had some sandwiches and tea and coffee. All our watches and mobile phones and cash and other belongings were in a heap in the middle of the table and we spent a few minutes sorting them out. When we were all settled Toby told us his story.

"All this started a very long time ago", said Toby, "long before I joined the organisation."

4

Pedro Vargas was born in Brazil in the northern coastal city of Salvador. His parents were middle-class intellectuals, his father was headmaster of one of the best secondary schools in the city and his mother was employed in local government where she was in charge of a group of care-homes for destitute old people. Pedro and his identical twin brother Orlando were brought up in a pleasant house in a leafy suburb of Salvador, which is the capital of the state of Bahia, an enormous area of fertile land stretching for hundreds of miles inland, westward from the Atlantic coast. The beaches on the coast are superb stretches of white sand and the two little boys grew up brown and fit and happy.

Happy, that is, until their parents were drowned in a ferry accident crossing the Baia de todos os Santos when the twins were only six years old. The accident occured on a Friday afternoon when the ferry was run down by a freighter in thick fog and sank immediately. Forty-seven passengers were drowned including the Vargas parents.

The twins were adopted by a brother and sister of their father by agreement with all the members of the family. This meant that the twins were separated which must have been traumatic for both of them and in hindsight was clearly a great mistake.

Pedro was adopted by his uncle Ramos who lived on a farm near the town of Luís Eduardo Magalhães in the far west of the state of Bahia. The farm had been developed by Ramos's father and was large, even by Brazilian standards. Ramos and his wife Adriana were childless so there were no cousins for Pedro to play with, but the gauchos and farm-hands had dozens of kids and he soon joined in with their activities.

Orlando was adopted by his aunt Maria who was married to a lawyer and lived in a spacious apartment right in the centre of Salvador. She had three daughters of her own, the youngest of whom Henriqueta was a few years older than Orlando, and Orlando rubbed along alright with his cousins who on the whole treated him quite kindly. From the beginning Maria had drummed in to her children how awful it must have been for little Orlando to lose both his parents. Nevertheless Orlando was self-reliant and spent a lot of his time on his own to begin with.

Pedro was bright and quick to learn and was soon flourishing at the local school and spending all his spare time learning about the farm and the countryside. He became a brilliant horseman and expert with machinery too so that Ramos grew immensely proud of Pedro and loved him like a son. One day all this will be yours, Ramos thought wryly to himself, and he schooled and directed Pedro accordingly without saying anything to him.

Orlando did not excel at any subjects at school except mathematics where he was head and shoulders above his peers. He was an attractive boy and he grew in confidence so that he soon became leader of a gang of boys at school and in the surrounding neighbourhood. He was a dare-devil and like all such kids he drew a crowd of admirers around him. They played on the beaches and in the parks and streets and his exploits became legendary, climbing up the sides of buildings and walking along parapets six or seven stories high with no fear. He was also a fierce and talented boxer.

When he reached puberty Orlando developed into a beautiful young man with a body like an Adonis, and one night his cousin Henriqueta seduced him. But he found this a painful experience because his foreskin was too tight, so Henriqueta took him to a rabbi who circumcised him and Henriqueta nursed him through the weeks of resultant pain and embarrasment and when he had recovered she taught him to make love to her and she secretly visited his bedroom most nights. One of the results of this was that Orlando never joined in the smutty jokes and innuendos of his young friends, though he kept the reason to himself. Eventually Henriqueta left home to go to college in Rio de Janeiro but she and Orlando always remained good friends.

Pedro grew up and when he was twenty years old he got to know Catarina who was the daughter of Ramos's old friend and neighbour Hernando da Silva. Catarina lived for horses and was a wonderful rider so she and Pedro soon became inseperable and she taught him to break and school young horses. She set her cap at Pedro who soon fell under her spell and in the fullness of time they were married. Catarina was an only child and her father was immensely wealthy, he owned a shipping company and coal and tin mines as well as several large estates.

It was obvious that eventually Pedro and Catarina would one day jointly own a vast fortune and Ramos and Hernando made sure that Pedro was capable of managing it. He soon demonstrated his talent for business and the two elder statesmen were able to relax. Pedro and Catalina had five children, so succession was guaranteed.

Meanwhile Orlando resisted all attempts by his aunt Maria and her respectable husband to train him for a professional career and he slowly drifted away from them into a life of easy living and crime. He was a born leader and used to organising other people so he set up a network selling crack cocaine to start with and later the powdered form, in the streets of Salvador.

The problem with drug rings is that they are extremely territorial and crossing boundaries leads to fights between gangs. There were several unexplained deaths in Salvador and the police started to become aware of Orlando's activities so that he moved to Rio de Janeiro for a while until one night after a shoot-out he had to flee over the border into Uruguay. Nothing was heard of him for twenty years, it was as if he had vanished off the face of the earth.

Pedro built up the family investments into a global operation, increasing their value by acquiring related businesses which fitted into the pattern of primary production in mining, agriculture and forestry. Ramos and Hernando died within a year of each other content in the knowledge that their hard work had been worthwhile. But, just after Pedro and Catarina's silver wedding celebrations Catarina was killed in a riding accident, which utterly devastated Pedro. Standing at the graveside after Catarina was buried Pedro looked up into the eyes of the stranger who had come up to him. It was just like looking into a mirror.

"Olà, my brother", said Orlando and he clasped Pedro to him.

"How did you come to be here?" asked Pedro, when he recovered from his surprise.

"I read about Catarina on the internet", said Orlando, "and I thought it was time to come and make your aquaintance after all these years. I am sorry for your loss"

"Come back to my place for some refreshments", said Pedro, and they drove back slowly to his house where Pedro introduced him to all and sundry as his prodigal brother.

"Stay a while", said Pedro in his generous way after the wake, so Orlando settled into a comfortable way of life as a house guest. He soon insinuated himself into Pedro's world and Pedro showed him absolutely everything to do with the family organisation, and he met all the managers and business people who came and went during the course of the weeks.

After a while Orlando told Pedro he would have to be moving on and despite Pedro's protestations and offers of a business partnership he left one morning to return to Uruguay.

"Adios, adios", was all he said as he disappeared in his car, raising dust from the track as he drove off.

A couple of weeks later Pedro received a phone call from Orlando. He was in a motel about forty miles away, he hadn't returned to Uruguay after all. He was in bad trouble and he needed Pedro's help. Could Pedro came and see him and bring some cash with him, maybe a thousand dollars.

"Don't tell anyone where you're going or who you're going to visit", begged Orlando, and Pedro promised he would say nothing to anybody. He was worried about his twin brother.

Pedro got a couple of thousand dollars out of his safe and filled up his Landcruiser with gasoline at the farm pump and set off to the motel to meet Orlando. As he was approaching the township he saw Orlando in the centre of the road waving him down. Orlando jumped into the vehicle and asked Pedro to pull off the road at the next turning on the left. They drove up a track to a deserted farmstead which had been abandoned several year ago. Orlando got out of the Landcruiser and went into the dilapidated house and Pedro followed. Orlando stood aside to let Pedro go into what had once been the kitchen and as he walked into the centre of the room Orlando shot him in the back of the head with a revolver he had stolen from Pedro's armoury.

Orlando dragged Pedro's body into the next room and took off the jacket and trousers. He replaced them with his own and left all his own identification papers, bank cards and bits and pieces in the pockets. Then he pushed Pedro's body down the steps into the cellar. He spent the rest of the day paving over the floor above the cellar and the trapdoor with old slabs he had previously gathered ready for the purpose and was careful to rub old dirt and dust into the gaps in between the stones to make it look as if they had been there for years.

One day someone may find Orlando Vargas's body, he thought. No-one will even pause to ask why he wasn't circumcised because there's nobody who knows that little fact.

Driving back as Pedro Vargas he carried out the final part of his plan. The Landcruiser crashed into a tree and his face and right hand were quite badly injured. He was surprised how much the self-inflicted wounds hurt but when a passing neighbour stopped to offer help and was concerned for him he was gratified to find that he passed off as his brother with no trouble at all. His speech was slightly slurred due to his swollen jaw, and he couldn't write very well with his injured hand over the next few weeks, but nobody thought twice about it. He cleaned the revolver and replaced it in the armoury and bit by bit he started to take stock of his new identity and all that went with it.

He went through all the accounts one by one. He was as rich as Croesus. Naturally the children of Catarina and Pedro would have a large chunk of the fortune but there would be plenty left over for him. He kept on with his master plan.

First he decided to dispose of the large holdings in industrial and mining and shipping stocks. He was able to do this discretely without causing any raised eyebrows because of Pedro's close relationship with a hedge fund manager operating out of Rio and New York. He left the agricultural and forestry investments intact for the next generation. These included meatworks and mills and timber yards. He put all the cash he had raised on deposit in a New York investment bank. Two and a half billion dollars.

He kept on with the support of the Brazilian Rainforest Conservation Charity and the Save the Children Fund as a smokescreen. Then he announced that he had decided to travel overseas on his own for a while to try and get over his grief at the loss of his wife, and he flew to Europe.

In Switzerland he established various bank accounts and set up trusts, into which he deposited most of the money from New York. He bought a flat in Monte Carlo and kept a low profile on the Riviera for a month or two. Then he moved to England and established himself in a flat in London and purchased a small estate in Sussex. There followed the aquisition of the Paradigm Hotel Group and Golf GB. All seemed well.

He had an added bonus when he met Jennifer de Candole, the divorced daughter of one of the top brass at The Royal and Ancient Golf Club of which he had become a member when he bought Golf GB. Jennifer had fallen madly in love with him and they had married soon after they met and already had a very young child and another on the way. This had cemented Vargas's respectability and entry into society.

Back in Brazil, some time after he had killed his brother and after he had left for his trip, developers moved into the deserted farmhouse where the murder had taken place, and bulldozers cleared the site. The hidden cellar was discovered and then the corpse with Orlando's identity in the pockets of the clothes.

The police tracked down Orlando's next of kin, and his cousin Henriqueta who was still unmarried and living in Rio on her own, was persuaded to travel out west to identify the body, expenses paid of course. She saw at once that the victim had not been circumcised and she

171

told the police that for that reason the body could not be that of Orlando Vargas, it must by process of elimination be that of Pedro Vargas.

The police were quite surprised that a middle-aged spinster lady would know such a thing but they didn't press the point with Henriqueta. Instead they confirmed the fact that the corpse was indeed that of Pedro by carrying out confidential DNA tests. Forensic tests also showed that the bullet which had killed Pedro had been fired from the revolver in the armoury at the farm.

Interpol was alerted and in due course Pedro aka Orlando Vargas was tracked down to Europe and then to England. But there was a problem with arranging his deportation to Brazil as there was no actual proof that Orlando had commited the murder, only circumstantial evidence which would not pass muster with the UK courts. The police and the authorities decided to watch Vargas closely and wait until he made a mistake or went back to Brazil on his own volition. They laid low.

5

Toby paused and poured himself a glass of water. He looked at me.

"We'd gathered enough evidence to move on Vargas and we were in the process of planning how to go about it when I got your email", he said. "This galvanised us into action so we pressed the green button and mobilised all our forces and that's why we're here", and he grinned at Alex.

"Toby and I had lunch in London shortly after Simon's sixtieth birthday party", said Alex, "and he told me about the coca plant and the million and a half euros, and the domes and other buildings in the quarry. This gave me enough ammunition to be able to launch an enquiry with the Drug Squad and we soon established that the laboratory in the quarry was processing tons of the stuff, some home-grown but most of it imported. We traced it all back to Vargas."

"As soon as I got your email we set 'Operation Marmalade Cat' in motion", Toby continued, "we simultaneously raided the quarry, Vargas's homes in Sussex and London and every club in the Golf GB group and every hotel in the Paradigm chain. Now we're searching *Tabebuia Alba*. We've got a massive haul of drugs and drug-making equipment and piles of stolen equipment and artefacts – enough to keep our recording and forensic teams busy for months and quite enough to put Vargas away for a very long time.

I expect the Brazilian authorities will be keen to question Vargas in due time. And to cap it all your brother Frank has handed over the million and a half euros in €500 notes which are very incriminating for Vargas because the European Central Bank will have a record of the serial numbers and what's more they'll be covered in Vargas's fingerprints. Frank told us he'd rather not have anything to do with them, he and Kate feel it's like blood money."

"Where is Vargas now?" asked Ellie.

"Safely tucked up in Paddington Green Police Station" answered Alex.

"Why on earth did Vargas come to England in the first place?" asked Brigid.

"Because we're just about the least regulated country in the western world", said Toby. "Also, we're part of Europe and a huge market of getting on for half a billion people. It was a natural place for him to come and set up a network of cocaine dealers. There are far too many people in England who have a cocaine habit, it's a huge recreational drug. People like footballers and film stars and city dealers all of whom have loads of cash".

Alex took up the thread. "England is the easiest place in Europe to launder money – provided you have enough of it – the regulations prevent the ordinary citizen but not the ultra-rich. That's why so many of the top premier league football teams are owned by wealthy foreign individuals, and London properties have been bought up by Russians and Chinese and Indians, and now Brazilians."

"Why doesn't the government do something about it then?" Brigid piped up again. She looked very indignant and I admired her feisty attitude.

"Well the government has completely lost control", answered Alex, "they're in thrall to the big money men who run the global businesses which dominate the markets, like the banks and the media and the phamaceuticals and the supermarkets and the oil companies. These and other world-wide organisations hold sway. They also evade taxes and they and their top management keep the bulk of their investments offshore. They're not answerable to anyone"

"Can't anyone do anything about it?"

"Our hopes lie with the silent majority. There are signs that they're stirring and with modern communications they can voice their opinions and take concerted action independantly of elected politicians. We're starting to see this with Occupy and the Arab Spring and Wikileaks and Facebook. The ordinary folk are getting fed up with the inertia of the politicians and are starting to take things into their own hands."

"There's also a large core of genuine dedicated people who do all the work", interjected Toby, "people who work in health and education and the police and the fire brigade, and the self-employed, and volunteers, all of whom have become very disenchanted with elected politicians in our so-called democracy."

There was a long silence while we thought this over.

"We mustn't get too serious", said Alex, "who'd like another drink?" and he looked around the table.

"I like a serious discussion" said Polly, "and I think one of the solutions is for more women to get involved with everything."

"Hear, hear", said Ellie and Brigid in unison and we all laughed.

"It's time for bed", said Alex, "we've all had a very long day. We'll have to be in touch with you guys to clear up some of the details, but thanks a lot for everything."

"No, thank you both and all your people" said Jake feelingly.

We gathered our things together and bid farewell to Toby and Alex and walked back to our digs. Jake spoke up on the way.

"I've been thinking", he said " and I suggest that Brigid and Ellie share the bed in our room and I'll curl up on a couple of sleeping bags on the floor". And so it was.

Chapter 9

1

Next day Jake and I sailed *Cinnabar Moth* back to Hayling Island and Polly drove Ellie and Brigid home via the ferry with all our gear. It was a bit of an anti-climax after the previous few days and it gave us time for reflection. We looked back at *Tabebuia Alba* riding on her mooring as we sailed eastwards towards Chichester Harbour and thought how lucky we were that everything had turned out alright. The alternative didn't bear thinking of.

We found our berth at Hayling Island marina and sorted out all the sails and ropes and sheets and stowed all the equipment. Then we turned off all the electronics and the gas and the engine fuel pipe and stuffed any rubbish into a bag for disposal ashore. I locked up the hatch with the padlock and we checked the mooring ropes once more and went to find my car. One of the tyres was as flat as a pancake and we had to change the wheel. Then the car wouldn't start so we had to find a member of the club to give us a jump start. Eventually we got going and I dropped Jake off at his home.

"Thanks for everything", said Jake "I've got a few things to sort out now, but I'll be in touch soon", and he blinked at me in a friendly way.

"So long", I said and drove off home.

On the way back I called in at the local garage and got them to fix the flat tyre. It needed a brand new tyre so I had two new ones put on the front wheels and the two next best on the rear wheels and kept the best of the others as a spare. Finally I got home. It was time to get back to normal.

Of course normal was much too much to expect and when I went into the kitchen I found my mother-in-law Camelia bustling around fixing things.

"Polly's pains have started", she said and gave me a warm kiss. "She's upstairs putting her things in a case. We've alerted the hospital, so you're just in time to take her in".

I left my cases and stuff dumped on the floor where I'd dropped them and went up the stairs two at a time. Polly looked at me calmly.

"Don't panic Mister Mannering", she said, "just help me wth the zip on this case".

The next twenty-four hours were a bit of a blur. Being the husband of a woman giving birth is quite hard. Oh, I know billions of babies have been born safely and I know that maternity departments are fantastic and I know it's much harder for the woman, but when someone you love is going through pain and suffering partly because of you, it's kind of hard to have to stand by and be stoical when you feel so helpless. Everything is being dealt with by others and you feel pretty useless too. And to cap it all Camelia was a qualified midwife.

Polly was amazing. And the baby was a healthy beautiful boy.

"You hold him", said Polly", and I took the tiny bundle in my arms and sat on the edge of Polly's bed. It was the most wonderful feeling.

"I'd like to call him Albert William", said Polly "after his two grandfathers".

It seemed a perfect solution.

"We'll leave out the 'de' from Adelbert of course, and anyway I expect he'll always be called either Bert or Bill anyway". She looked at me.

"Now you can kiss your son's mother", she said. And so I did.

2

By the time I went to fetch Polly and Bertie home the next day, Camelia and I had got everything ready for them both. Having Camelia there was a real bonus and I quite hoped that she would stay on for a bit to help look after Polly, but being the person she was she went back to Whitechapel the following day leaving Polly and me to get on with it.

"Adelbert and I will come down to stay for a week-end soon, when you've got into a routine," she said when I kissed her goodbye.

Pinky and Perky were highly suspicious of Bertie to start with but soon got used to him when they realised that he was no threat and wouldn't steal their bones.

We got into a routine quite quickly in fact. I decided to work in the dining room at home for a while so that I could be on hand to help Polly with anything she needed, so I brought home my laptop and printer and the files of the clients which needed to be worked on and just went into the office in Horsham from time-to-time to collect the post when I went to town to do any shopping. If I needed to see a client I could always visit them.

One morning I was working on a client's accounts and I got distracted into thinking about the Vargas saga. There were quite a lot of loose ends. For example, there must have been other people involved with the illegal businesses which were being run from Cottesloe Golf Club and from the quarry. I wondered who they were and what they would do now. And would the police follow-up all the threads? What would happen to the gangmasters who ran the artful dodgers? And what about the people working in the laboratory, how much if anything did they know? And besides what actually had been going on in the domes and in the lab? There were so many unanswered questions.

I couldn't concentrate on my client's affairs without committing all my thoughts on the Vargas saga to paper. I got out the current Moleskine notebook and started a new page. I wrote down the date and 'Vargas' at the top and drew a line underneath this heading. Then I tried as logically as possible to go through every part of all the activities with which Vargas had been involved, writing sub-headings and lists of items as they occurred to me. It took me a long time, but it was a kind of catharsis and once I had completed the job I was able to get back to working on my client's accounts without continually coming back to Vargas and just sitting staring into space.

"What have you been up to Holmes?" asked Polly when I went into the kitchen for some tea. It really was uncanny how she could read my mind. I told her what I'd been doing, while she fed Bertie. He was a greedy little chap but luckily Polly had plenty of milk and she'd taken to feeding Bertie like a duck takes to water. Instinct is a fantastic thing, I thought.

After tea I worked on the accounts of my new estate agent client, Abbott & King. The firm consisted of three partners each of whom specialised in one kind of property. Bruce Abbott was in charge of commercial property, his brother Joseph ran the residential division and their cousin Henry King was the agricultural specialist. They had racked up some pretty useful profits since they started the partnership and the spread of the types of properties they handled meant that they were less vulnerable to a recession than if they had specialised in only one kind. They had been prudent with their money too and had bought the freehold of their office building when they had saved up enough to purchase it without any debt. They had also bought several small commercial units on an estate outside Partridge Green for rental income.

I spent a while going through their sales invoices looking at the fees they had charged. I suddenly sat bolt upright.

I read the invoice again.

'Advising on the sale of 648 acres of grade 1 arable farmland to Mr Charles George Farley for £1.2 million. Fees £12,960 plus VAT, disbursements and advertising £1,875'.

What's Charley Farley doing buying farmland, I wondered. And where did he get £1.2 million from? I made a note and continued riffling through the invoices. Then I found another invoice to a different client.

'Advising on the sale of Coombelands Farm to Mr Charles George Farley for £3.8 million. Fees £34,000 plus VAT, disbursements and advertising £6,500'.

And there were four more sales of agricultural properties to Charley during the year. All in all he had bought nearly fifteen million quid's worth. I mentioned it to Henry King when I was at his office the next day.

"Charlie's been buying farmland for three years now", said Henry, "he can't get enough of it. He must have spent nearly forty million so far through us. I can give you the details if you like, we keep a tally of everything any purchaser buys so that we can offer them anything which comes on to the market, if they're a serious investor", and he browsed on his computer for a moment or two and printed me off a list of every property Charlie Farley had bought from clients of Abbott & King.

"We're not the only people he's bought through," said Henry, "I know for a fact that he's bought farms and land from clients of both Savills and Knight Frank."

"Good for him," I said but I secretly wondered where the hell he'd got the money from.

I got home at lunchtime and had a bowl of soup and home-made bread with Polly. Bertie was fast asleep in his cot, and Pinky and Perky were asleep by the Aga. It was a chilly day.

I told Polly what I had discovered about Charlie Farley.

"Well you always thought his books were too good to be true", said Polly. "I wonder how he's generated so much spare cash. Scrap metal must be worth a lot more than you'd think."

"Either that or he's involved in something else which doesn't go through the books of The Chaotic Scrap Metal and Recycling Company Limited." I said.

"Well, sooner or later you'll no doubt find out what it's all about," said Polly, then she went on "actually I've had some rather upsetting news this morning." She looked sad.

"What?" I asked.

"Tracy came round for a coffee and to see Bertie and to ask if there was anything she could do to help. As we were sitting down drinking our coffee she suddenly burst into tears. I've never seen her like that before and it took quite a while for her to recover enough to be able to talk to me. Then she told me that Andy and she have split up." Polly stopped and looked at me.

"How absolutely terrible," I said "I can't believe it. What on earth happened?"

"Well she's been wanting to have a baby for quite a long time now but to begin with Andy always said they needed a bit more security and regular income before they could start a family and then when at last he agreed they could try for a baby she didn't seem to be able to have one. Now Andy's gone and fallen for one of the young women vets in the local large animal practice and yesterday he told Tracy he was going to leave her and shack-up with this woman. She's completely distraught about it. Nothing I said could help."

"Is there any chance he'll think better of it and go back to Tracy?" I asked.

"Not at the moment," replied Polly "and besides Tracy says she wouldn't take him back now for all the tea in China. I feel awful about it and especially when I've got Bertie and you and I feel so happy, it just doesn't seem fair."

I loitered in the kitchen instead of going back into the dining room to get on with Abbott & King's accounts, which all of a sudden seemed rather unimportant. Bertie woke up and Polly fed him again and we took turns in holding him and trying to bring his wind up. Then I took Pinky and Perky out for a walk and we had a good blow along the footpath. There was a brisk sou'-westerly and the leaves were being blown off the trees. It was fun walking through the carpet of dried, dead leaves and it reminded me of walks in my childhood.

For the next few days I spent most of the time completing clients' accounts and preparing their individual self-assessment tax returns. These were pretty straight-forward and I had an excellent software package which calculated everything necessary, as long as the entries were accurate, and it meant I could file the returns with the Revenue on-line.

There were two clients whose tax returns presented a problem, Frank Waller and Charlie Farley. I needed to discuss the treatment of the loss of containers in the accounts of Southern Orchids with Frank, and I had to broach the problem of the purchases of farms and farmland with Charley. I arranged to see them both on the same day. In the meantime I had been asked to spend a day at a workshop with Rex and his dairy costings group in the lecture room at Brinsbury Agricultural college.

The workshop turned out to be very worthwhile. Rex organised his group of dairy farmers on quite strict lines and they clearly appreciated the trouble he took although they took the mickey out of him all the time. Each member of the group ran their herds on similar lines, based on a New Zealand system known as 'block-calving'. This involved calving all the cows at the same time of year in a tight group. There were several benefits of trying to achieve this, the main one being that you could concentrate on one main activity at a time throughout the year.

There were five items on the agenda for the day, cow fertility, grazing management, silage making and feeding, milk quality, and gross margin per acre. I realised that I'd been invited along so that I could learn as much about the system as possible and would be better able to give them good financial advice as a result. I certainly learnt a lot and really enjoyed the day. Afterwards we had a glass of beer and one of the farmers told a couple of really funny stories. I drove home in high spirits.

Next day I set off for my meetings with Frank and Charley. While driving along the Chichester bypass towards Southern Orchids it suddenly occurred to me that I had never actually been asked by Charley Farley to prepare his tax return, only to do the audit of The Chaotic Scrap Metal and Recycling Company Limited. Before I launched into a whole bunch of questions about his land purchases I had better make sure of my position. Otherwise I would not only look stupid but I might stir up a hornet's nest at the same time.

Frank Waller was his usual friendly self when I arrived at the nursery.

"How are you?" he asked, "a lot of water's passed under the bridge since I last saw you", and he ushered me into the office where the table had been laid up for coffee and there was a fruit cake on a plate in the middle of the table.

"It's my birthday actually", said Frank, "so Kate thought we should have a piece of cake with our coffee", and he proceeded to cut a couple of large slices from the cake and handed me a plate with one of them on it, followed by a cup of coffee.

"Thanks very much," I said, "and please thank Kate – oh and happy birthday too." I grinned at him as I sipped the coffee. "What shall we do about the loss of containers?" I asked him.

"Well I've thought about it a lot," said Frank "and I think we should just write the whole thing off to experience, don't you?" I waited for him to go on.

"I expect Toby and Alex told you I'd handed over the euros to them. Kate and I just decided we couldn't have anything to do with them, besides €500 notes aren't legal tender in the UK anyway I gather. It's a hell of a big hit to write-off but we've been extremely lucky with the business and we can stand it if we're careful and carry on working hard. I just got a huge contract for orchids from Wyvern Garden Centres, I had to clear the deal with Robinsons first but they were quite happy about it. They take the view that competition never hurt anybody and the more people get used to buying orchids the better. What do you think?" and he looked at me straight in the eyes as he always did.

"That's exactly how I saw it," I said, "the only caveat is that if you ever do decide to use any of those euros – after all they're yours not the government's – then you'll have to include them in your accounts as income and it'll go straight to the bottom line if you do. I'll make a note on your file for you to sign if you agree." Frank nodded.

"Of course," he said "you've got to cover yourself." He grinned again. "Now I want to ask you a favour," he said.

"What's that?" I asked.

"Well we've formed the tree nursery into a charitable trust and Kate and I thought you might like to be a trustee on the board – actually Kate wondered if you'd agree to be the chairman of trustees. Chichester County Council will have a representative on the board of trustees too, but we thought you'd make a good chairman. What do you think?".

"I'd be glad to." I said.

"That's great," said Frank and he grasped my hand firmly. "Have you got time for lunch before you go?"

"I'd better be getting on," I said "I've got to see another client immediately after lunch and he's an hour's drive away, but thanks all the same." I got up to go.

"Send me the papers to sign, please," said Frank "and your bill, and I'll sign everything and send it back with a cheque", and he saw me to the door. He waved as I drove out of the nursery car park. What a brilliant client, I thought, I wish they were all like him.

I stopped at the Chalet Café, a greasy spoon outside Cowfold, for some lunch. I ordered bacon and eggs and a pot of tea, and sat half reading the paper and half mulling over my meeting with Frank and the upcoming one with Charley. The Chalet Café was a very popular eating house with lots of local as well as passing trade.

On Sunday mornings it was frequented both by bikies, and by the police either going off duty or coming on duty who met for breakfast to pass on any information. The sight of squad cars parked in a row alongside Harley Davidsons and Nortons was incongruous to say the least. Inside it was the same, leather jackets and pony tails alongside yellow tops. One of the better sides of Britain, I thought.

Later, as I drove through the security gates of The Chaotic Scrap Metal and Recycling Company Limited I saw a huge crane with its boom poised over the rear of the scrapyard. It was lowering a massive metal structure into place.

"That's our new crushing plant," said Charley as I got out of the car, "the business is growing so fast we need to quadruple our crushing capacity," and he turned his head towards me and his dark glasses shone in the sun. I wondered what colour his eyes were, I'd never yet seen them. He turned and led the way into the office and shut the door. The noise outside was cut off immediately.

"Can't hear yourself think out there," said Charley and pointed to a chair for me to sit in opposite him at his desk. As usual the place was littered with papers and manuals and trade magazines.

"I've brought the final accounts of the company for you and Peg to sign," I said "and various schedules and statements as well. Then I can file the accounts at Companies House and with the Revenue. Here's the corporation tax computation, the figure at the bottom is what you'll have to pay in due course," and I passed it over to him. He looked at it and grunted.

He's a pig, I thought, just a bloody pig, and I felt quite amused as it had been bothering me for some time what it was that Charley reminded me of.

"Do you want me to do your personal tax returns?" I asked.

"Not necessary lad," said Charley "Peg does all that. I'll get her to come in and we can sign everything up for you." He grabbed his iPhone and pressed the button. Peg appeared as if by magic a couple of minutes later. She seemed larger than ever. Just like a sow about to farrow, I thought ungraciously.

"Hullo love," she said to me, and plonked herself down on an upturned crate. Her bottom sagged over the edge of the crate on each side. She wiped a strand of dyed blond hair away from her eyes and looked at Charley expectantly. I stared fascinated at the line of dark hair in the parting at the top of her head.

They both signed everything without demur, including a statement confirming that the accounts were not only in accordance with the books but that everything was included and nothing had been omitted and that there were no other items at the date of the accounts or since which would in any way have affected or altered the accounts.

I then presented my bill for the amount which we had agreed when I took them on as clients.

"Is there a discount for cash?" asked Charley.

"Charley Farley you are the bleedin' limit", gushed Peg and she got the company cheque book out of a drawer and wrote and signed a cheque for the full amount.

"And thanks to you, love," she said and handed me the cheque.

"That's OK," I replied "see you next year", and I gathered up all my stuff and said goodbye.

While I was driving home from The Chaotic Scrap Metal and Recycling Company Limited I felt quite relieved that I hadn't got to do the Farleys' tax returns. It meant I didn't need to delve into their personal finances or ask any awkward questions about purchases of farmland or any other issues. I said as much to Polly.

"No," she said "you may not have to but someone should. Charlie Farley is right up there as a member of the criminal classes, otherwise how on earth has he got hold of millions and millions of pounds? You never know, he might have been bound up in all that Vargas stuff, after all he's in the scrap and recycling business and he could easily be involved in drugs as well." She looked at me with her school-ma'm face.

"So, what should I do?" I asked her.

"You should tell Toby what you know and let him decide whether he thinks he ought to take it any further," she replied, "after all he did a brilliant job with Vargas."

I mulled it over. I wasn't really a whistleblower or a tell-tale at heart. It was much more my style to let sleeping dogs lie. Nevertheless I knew that Polly had a sixth sense about lots of things and there was little doubt that Charley and Peg were up to something crooked, unless they'd inherited a fortune or won the lottery in which case they had nothing to hide. I had felt uneasy about them ever since the first day I'd met them. I agreed that I would call Toby the next day.

When I rang Toby he sounded rather formal on the telephone. Before I could even begin to tell him why I had rung he said he'd like to meet up and when would it be convenient. I guessed there was someone else in the room with him or that maybe our conversation was being recorded or was being listened in to.

"It's quite a while since we last saw each other," he said "and I haven't met my little cousin Albert yet, how would it be if I came down this week-end and spent the night? I'd like to bring my partner too."

"That would be lovely," I replied, matching his tone, "come down together in time for tea on Saturday and we can catch up with all our family news."

"Great, thanks," was all he said and he rang off.

I told Polly about my conversation with Toby and she seemed very pleased that we were going to see him again. She was also intrigued about Toby's 'partner' and wondered who it was.

"Maybe he's gay," I said.

"Anything's possible," replied Polly.

For most of that week I wrestled with the accounts of my new solicitor clients. Widgerys was a small firm of solicitors with two women parners. They specialised in family law although they would also undertake a minimal amount of additional work for their clients if asked. Anything that was outside family law they passed on to other specialist firms. They were both sympathetic people and attracted quite a large clientele of mainly women.

The real problem with all solicitors' accounts is clients' money. This has to be kept in a separate bank account designated 'Client Account' at all times and clients' money must in no way get into the firm's own bank account. If it does then it is the duty of the auditor to report the matter to the Law Society. Fortunately the partners at Widgerys were well aware of all this and everything was in good shape. By the end of the week I was ready to sign everything off.

4

Toby arrived just before teatime on Saturday in his new black VW Golf. Polly and I looked out of the kitchen window and watched him park the car. It was a simply beautiful early winter's day with a clear blue sky and not a breath of wind. There was a nip in the air. There'll be a frost tonight, I thought to myself.

Toby got out of the car and came round to the rear and opened the boot. This obscured the far side of the car so we weren't able to see who the passenger was.

Eventually the person got out. You could have knocked us over with a feather. It was Ellie.

Toby and Ellie came into the kitchen, he was carrying a couple of cases and Ellie had a bunch of friesias for Polly which she gave her after they'd hugged each other. Suddenly we all started talking at once. The noise was deafening and Bertie woke up and started to cry. This meant that Ellie and Toby had to be introduced to Bertie, and Polly had to sit down and feed him, and I fussed around making tea, and Toby and Ellie stood holding hands, looking ridiculously happy.

Bit by bit the story came out as we sat and drank our tea and ate hot buttered crumpets.

After the rescue from *Tabebuia Alba* Toby and Alex had interviewed Ellie to obtain as much detail as possible from her concerning everything she knew about the Vargas organisation. This then led to several long meetings alone between Toby and Ellie because Alex had had to go to Manchester after two days to start work on a new and urgent case. One thing had led to another and it gradually dawned on Toby and Ellie that they were enjoying these question and answer sessions so much that they didn't want them to end.

"We just realised we were in love," said Ellie "and we wanted to be together all the time."

"So we have been ever since," confirmed Toby.

"What about Jake?" asked Polly.

"Oh, he's tied up with Brigid," said Ellie "and besides he and I decided to accept an offer to sell Jakellie Recycling, so he's been frantically busy tidying everything up and getting it ready to hand it over to the new owners. He's pretty happy with the arrangement, the purchasers have taken a short lease on the property and have agreed to keep everyone on, they may even recruit more apprentices because they reckon the business will expand."

What'll he do now it's sold?" I asked.

"He's hell bent on starting up a new venture designing and manufacturing equipment to help make handicapped people's lives better. Things like mobility, and remote controls to act as substitute hands, and easier communications. He's got masses of ideas. There's a guy called Trevor Baylis who invented the wind-up radio and made millions out of it and who now helps other inventors patent and market their ideas and he's helping Jake. I'm sure Jake'll want Tom to look after the accounts and other stuff when he gets it going."

We cleared away the tea things and Polly showed Ellie and Toby to their room. Then we all got dressed in coats and scarves and wellington boots and went for a good walk. Polly carried Bertie in the bushbaby and walked with Ellie, and I looked after Pinky and Perky and walked alongside Toby. He told me about his parents' latest trip, looking for plants in Slovenia.

"Apparently it's the most beautiful and unspoilt country," said Toby, "they want to go back again as soon as possible, probably in the spring to see the wild meadow flowers. Then they plan to go to New Zealand next to see the tree ferns."

"They're obviously enjoying Simon's retirement," I said, and Toby nodded.

We were quite a long way ahead of Polly and Ellie by now. I let Pinky and Perky off their leads and they ran off into the bushes. We walked on along the footpath.

Toby said "What was it you rang me about the other day?"

I told him all about my suspicions concerning Charley and Peg Farley and the fact that all their records were in apple pie order but that they'd bought millions of pounds worth of farms and farmland and that the whole thing just didn't ring true. I also mentioned that Polly thought that the Farleys could have been tied up in some way with Vargas.

"That's why we decided to get in touch with you," I said.

"What's the name of the scrapyard?" asked Toby.

"The Chaotic Scrap Metal and Recycling Company Limited," I replied. Toby laughed.

"That's the name of the company which has bought Jakellie Recycling," he said "they paid cash up front for ninety percent of the business and there'll be a sweetener when they pay the balance if the stock is what Jake reckons it is. He's spending this week-end putting the finishing touches to a complete stocktake and valuation. The purchaser didn't want any certified accounts or anyone to know about the deal until it was completed."

We walked along in silence. One of my cousin's most attractive qualities was that he didn't talk too much. I wondered what we should do next and I was just about to say so when Toby broke the silence.

"Did you know that the District Council found out about the buildings in the quarry and put a demolition order on everything as there was no planning consent for any of it? It's all got to go within four weeks. There'll be nothing left by the end of the month. It looks like a bombsite at the moment. My department has had a heap of problems with the Council, we needed a lot of forensic samples and precise measurements but the Council was very uncooperative. We only managed to get what we wanted through my Minister's direct intervention. It seemed as if the Chief Executive of the Council almost had a personal interest in getting rid of the site."

"Maybe he did," I replied, "nothing would surprise me after everything that's happened during the last few months," and I laughed and looked at Toby. He looked rather solemn.

"We won't mention any of this during the week-end," he said "you can tell Polly about it after we've left on Sunday. I'll make some enquiries on Monday and I'll keep you informed of anything I find out. The fewer people who know about all this the better, just for now."

At this moment Pinky and Perky put up a rabbit and chased it into the undergrowth so I had to go after them and put them on a lead again in case they ran into the road a bit further on. By the time we got back home from our walk it was pitch dark.

Polly had cooked a wonderful pheasant casserole with root vegetables and cabbage and mashed potato and Toby prduced a bottle of Australian Shiraz so we ate our supper in the kitchen after Polly had put Bertie to bed in his cot. Pinky and Perky were in their usual positions in front of the Aga.

"Where did you get the pheasants?" asked Ellie "they're absolutely delicious."

"Andy Wilmot dropped them in yesterday," replied Polly "he had been on a shoot at Goodwood and had about half a dozen of them so he thought we might like a brace. I think he really came round to have a chat."

"I suppose you know about Andy and Tracy?" said Ellie.

"Yes we do actually," replied Polly, "and I still can't believe it," and she was silent for quite a while.

After supper, when we'd cleared away we played Scrabble, still sitting at the kitchen table as it was so warm and pleasant there. Toby was very competitive and he played a mean game and won quite easily with a final seven letter word which finished all his letters as well so he got a bonus. We had cups of cocoa and Horlicks and some Anzac biscuits which Polly had made the previous day and eventually we all trooped upstairs to bed, yawning contentedly.

Next Monday I went over to Billingshurst to start work on the audit of my new client Uni-Welding Limited. This was a new business in that it was the result of a management buyout of the welding division of the Unipart Group, which in the dim and distant past had been the parts division of British Leyland. Now Unipart had reinvented itself as a logistics company and it had got rid of all the bits of the business which didn't fit into its new corporate plan.

Uni-Welding had been bought by three young members of the division, who had scraped together enough money to put down a forty percent deposit for the purchase and had borrowed the rest from their bank. The story of how they'd got hold of the money for the deposit would have made a great case study for any business school. Each of the owners had mortgaged themself up to the hilt and they had borrowed from friends and relations and agreed with their partners to live on the smell of an oily rag until the deposit moneys were paid off. Now in its second year it was beginning to make a profit.

The business itself was very simple. It sold portable welding and cutting equipment to end-users through a network of distributors, mainly in the motor and agricultural trades. The machines themselves were imported from Italy and China. It was like the razor blade business in that once a customer had bought a machine they had to buy the rods and wire and protective gear and all the other kit and kaboodle from Uni-Welding so that there was continual recurring business. It was this aspect which had persuaded the bank to lend sixty percent of the purchase price.

The company had a good website which made it easy for a potential customer to be referred to the nearest distributor for a sale. It was the company's policy not to sell direct so that there would be no conflict of interest. Most of the energy of the management was spent in developing the distribution network and in supporting the distributors with service and stock and training.

I arrived at the company's premises and parked in the visitors' car park. The three owners were waiting for me in their open-plan office. One of them was a young woman called Christine Karell. The other two were blokes, Neil Harrington and Jonathan Arbuthnot. They showed me around the warehouse, explained the stock arrangements and gave me a quick overview of the computer system. Then we had a cup of tea and they suggested that Chris should take me to their nearest distributor which was in Burgess Hill, so that I could spend some time there examining their systems and look at the stock.

"We sell everything to the distributors on sale-or-return," said Neil "so we have to know exactly what the stock position is at each outlet. This is then compared with the stock shown on our computer. There are seldom any differences but you need to understand the way it works before you can do the audit properly." I nodded, it seemed like a very sensible idea.

I said goodbye for now and went out to my car and followed Chris in her car to Burgess Hill.

The distributors were on the Victoria Road industrial estate. Chris introduced me to the manager and after a short interval she left to get back to headquarters. I spent an hour or two looking at the systems and the stocks of equipment and peripherals which related to the firm's dealings with Uni-Welding, which only represented about a fifth of its total trade. It was very straightforward and after I'd made a few notes and satisfied myself that I understood the set-up between the two businesses I said goodbye and drove off back to the Horsham office. I called Neil Harrington and told him I'd had a good look at everything and arranged to go back to Billingshurst the following week to complete the Uni-Welding audit.

I sat in the office and went through the post and listened to the messages on the answerphone. Then I switched on my computer and checked my emails. I made a cafetière of coffee and made the usual sort of notes about Uni-Welding in the current Moleskine notebook. I thumbed through the notebook after I'd finished the notes, looking idly at the other entries for the previous period.

Something caught my eye and I went to the fireproof safe and got out the two previous notebooks. Then I took down the local Ordnance Survey map from the bookshelf, and dug out the schedule of the farms which had been purchased by Charlie Farley and which had been given to me by Henry King.

I spent a long time with a pencil, ringing round Charlie's farms and marking other places on the map, including the Cottesloe golf course and the quarry, and The

Chaotic Scrap Metal and Recycling Company Limited, as well as Jakellie Recycling and and Chemco Solutions. Then I marked all the places I could remember where the local gangmasters had had their teams of people picking fruit and veg. All roads lead to Rome, I thought, only in this case Rome was Charley Farley.

I called Toby and left a message for him to call me back as soon as possible. Then I put everything back in the safe.

I rang Polly and told her I was in the Horsham office and about to come home and I asked her if there was anything we needed in the shops. She gave me a short list and I walked up West Street towards Waitrose. I looked in the shop windows as I strolled along and wondered what on earth I could get Polly for her Christmas present.

6

Toby called me on my mobile soon after I got home.

"Is that you cousin?" he asked and I realised that this was code for me not to say anything important on the phone.

"Yes," I replied "how are you?"

"Fine thanks, what did you call about?" he said.

"I just rang you to let you know that I dug out the details of the holiday place I was talking about the other day and I've got a map to go with it," I went on. "Would you like me to send them to you or can you pick them up sometime?"

"I'm actually coming to Gatwick Airport tonight to collect my parents", he said "could you possibly meet me there?"

"Yes of course," I said, " it would be lovely to see Georgina and Simon too."

"Then I'll text you to arrange a meeting place when the train leaves East Croydon on the way to the airport," he said, and promptly rang off.

Shortly afterwards I got a text message: *See you in the car park of the Boars Head at nine tonite.*

The Boar's Head pub was on the Worthing Road leading out of Horsham on the western side of town, on the corner of the turning to Christ's Hospital School. This meant that Toby must be coming by car. I wonder if he just loves cloak and dagger stuff, I thought, or whether there's a real danger that someone might overhear us and that this might cause a problem.

I got to the pub car park slightly before nine and saw that Toby's VW Golf was parked there already. He got out of the car as I drew up, opened the passenger door of my car and jumped in.

"Please take me to your office," he said and sat down low in the seat until we got to Sainsbury's car park. When he got out of the car I saw that he had wound a scarf round his neck covering the lower part of his features and that he was wearing a slouch hat pulled well down over his face. It was pitch dark except for the street lights. I almost laughed when I saw what Toby looked like but luckily I stopped myself just in time.

When we got into my office and I had drawn the curtains Toby visibly relaxed and asked if I had anything he could eat.

"I've had nothing all day," he said. I looked in the fridge and in the biscuit tin and found some cheese and biscuits and a few tomatoes and made a cup of coffee for each of us.

"What have you found out?" asked Toby as he munched away at the food. I got all the papers out of the safe and went through them with him, explaining the significance of each item. He spent ages going through them all over and over again.

"Can I hang on to these for a while please?" he asked.

"Sure," I replied, at which he scooped up all the papers and stuffed them into the inside pocket of his trenchcoat.

"How's Polly?" he asked and when I said she was fine and asked him how Ellie was he nodded vigorously several times and then he seemed to go into a reverie.

"Can we go back to my car now, please?" he said eventually and I opened the office door and led the way outside after turning out the light and then I locked up and we went back to my car. I drove Toby back to collect his car and he galvanised himself enough to clasp me by the hand and then he muttered "this could all be very dodgy," jumped out of my car without a backward glance, unlocked his car, got in quickly and drove off without turning on the headlights until he was out in the main road. It was quite one of the weirdest exhibitions I had ever seen. By the time I had collected myself and driven out onto the Worthing Road his car had completely disappeared.

I drove home and found Polly sitting in the kitchen feeding Bertie, with Pinky and Perky once again in their usual places in front of the Aga. The radio was on low, I remember it was B*ook at bedtime*. It was a reassuring domestic scene. I put the kettle on to make a cup of tea.

I told Polly about my curious encounter with Toby and I chuckled when I described his get-up and his strange antics.

"He was only trying to shield you from any possible harm," said Polly looking stern, "he doesn't want any trouble for us. Toby knows what the criminal classes are really like. They'll stop at nothing to make sure they don't get caught. Just don't get involved other than to keep passing information on to Toby or Alex. We don't have a clue what's really going on. Keep on working at building up the practice and helping your clients and enjoying family life." She looked at me. There was a long pause.

"On that score," she said "I hope it's OK but I've invited Mum and Dad to spend Christmas with us, they've both been working such long hours at the hospital they'll need a good break."

"That'll be great," I said. I was very fond of my parents-in-law. They were interesting, and fun too. "What size turkey should we get?" I asked.

"Well funnily enough Andy called in again today and he told me that a farmer friend of his near Cranleigh has the most brilliant turkeys, just a few but they're organically reared and not too expensive as there's no middle man, so I ordered one of about nine or ten kilos oven-ready."

"What's Andy up to?" I asked.

"Well it's all over with the vet woman and Andy's desperate to get back with Tracy but she won't even talk to him she's so hurt. I think he's trying to use me as a conduit to stay in touch with Tracy. She's coming over for a coffee tomorrow morning so I'll see what happens when I tell her the latest about Andy. Now," she said "it's past our bed time," and she picked up Bertie and carried him towards the stairs. "Can you put the dogs round for a last pee," she went on, "and then come to bed. I need a cuddle."

I didn't need asking twice.

Later, in the small hours, I had another of my dreadful nightmares. I was in the office at The Chaotic Scrap Metal and Recycling Company Limited looking out of the window at Polly and Bertie who were sitting in the passenger seat of my Mini Cooper. Suddenly the JCB with the telescopic grab came roaring round the corner. It was being driven by Peg and I could see a ferocious look of rage on her face as she manoevred the vehicle up to the Mini, grabbed the car in the jaws of the JCB and drove it at full speed round the corner towards the crushing plant. I dragged myself out of my chair and ran out of the door only to see the grab poised over the top of the bin and lowering the Mini into the grinding mechanism. My legs were leaden and I was unable to move or scream or do anything at all, I felt completely impotent.

I woke up in a sweat, shaking from head to toe and only slowly did it dawn on me that I had been dreaming again. It took me ages to calm down and I had to get out of bed as quietly as possible so as not to disturb Polly and I crept over to Bertie's cot to make sure he was alright. He was lying on his back with his arms above his head, fast asleep. I went into the bathroom and dried myself off and sat on the edge of the bath and tried to relax.

I really need to see the doctor, I thought. I'll arrange an appointment with Doctor Nathan. But I decided not to say anything to Polly. Eventually I went back to bed and fell into a dreamless sleep.

7

During the period running up to Christmas I spent quite a lot of time working on the template for the presentation of the accounts for the dairy farmers in Rex's group. My idea was to show the financial results in such a way that they linked with Rex's costings statements and so that it would also be easy to compare the results of one herd with another without having to alter any of the format or layout. I prepared a draft and emailed it to Rex for his comments.

Everything was quiet on the Jakellie front and I didn't hear a peep from Charlie Farley either. I managed to finish the accounts of Uni-Welding and of Abbott &

King and of Widgerys and got them all signed off so as to have the decks cleared for the new year.

The bank manager rang to ask me out for a Christmas lunch during the first week of December and he took me to Côte which was always reliable. He actually seemed to be quite a good bloke and not one of your archetypal bank managers. He liked to get around to see his customers and always seemed genuinely interested in new ideas and start-ups. He was also well up on fraud and was keen to let you know the latest scams.

"Identity theft is getting out of control." he said "The latest con is to make a bogus phone call to a customer asking them to log on to their bank accounts while you keep them on the line and then talk them through installing a new piece of security software. This is the very opposite of secure, of course, and it allows the fraudster to get the details of the customer's log-in and password. Then they take all the money out of the account. It's as simple as that."

He got up to pay the bill and when this was done we sauntered down East Street past all the other retaurants and on into the Carfax where we were due to go in different directions. I stopped to thank him very much for lunch.

"No problem," he said " happy Christmas and New Year," and he turned as if he was about to walk back towards the bank, then he changed his mind and turned back and came and stood very close to me. He looked down at the kerb.

"A little bird told me that one of your clients has bought Cottesloe Golf Course," he said. "Here's a piece of free advice. It might be for the best if your wife doesn't go walking the dogs there in future."

"Why on earth not?" I asked. "Anyway, who is it that's bought it?"

He carried on looking at the pavement as if he was examining it minutely.

"Ah," he said "that'd be telling," then he smiled and put his hand on my shoulder and gave it a little squeeze and quickly walked away. I had half a mind to run after him and grab his arm and get him to tell me who it was but I didn't. I just stood there thinking. Then I walked on through the Carfax and across Albion Way to the surgery for my appointment with Doctor Nathan.

I sat in the waiting room waiting to be called, thinking about what the bank manager had said. Suddenly I looked up and saw that Doctor Nathan was standing looking at me and he waved his hand and beckoned me to follow him into his consulting room.

"How are you?" said the doctor after I'd taken off my coat and sat down in the chair next to his desk. He got my details up on his computer screen and peered at them and then transferred his gaze to me. He was very young and fit looking. His parents were from Kerala in South India but he'd been born and brought up and educated in Nottingham. He was an exceptionally gifted doctor.

I told him about my nightmares. He didn't laugh or dismiss them lightly. Instead he asked me to take off my sweater and shirt and he examined me thoroughly. Then he got his stethoscope out of his drawer and listened to my chest and my back and asked me to breathe in and out deeply, and then he took my blood pressure. He tapped on the keys of his computer.

"How's little Albert?" he asked.

"He's fine thanks," I replied.

"So are you actually," he said. "I don't think you need to worry about your health. I'm not very keen on prescribing sleeping tablets except for someone who has a genuine problem getting to sleep, which you don't have. Is there something which is worrying you particularly or which you're afraid of? This can sometimes cause a series of nightmares. You may be nervous about Albert, first-time parents can often be very anxious about infants."

"Maybe that's it," I said, suddenly thinking I was being rather pathetic.

"Are you taking any exercise?" asked Doctor Nathan.

"Not really," I replied, "I go for reasonably long walks whenever I can, but nothing more, I used to do a lot of rowing when I was at school and at university."

"Have you thought of doing yoga?" he asked "my wife teaches yoga locally. It's very good for you, as well as stretching you and making you breathe properly it has a spiritual element to it and can be very beneficial for stress as a result. Take one of Arundhati's cards and think about it." and he handed me a card with a photograph of an amazingly beautiful woman on it, with details of the place and times of the classes.

"I'll certainly think about it," I said "and thanks for seeing me, I'm sorry to waste your time."

"Now look here," said Doctor Nathan "don't ever think you're wasting my time and do come back and see me again if the dreams persist." Then I put my clothes back on again and thanked him very much and went out through the waiting room and walked back to the office. It was quite reassuring to get a check up every now and then and besides I really liked Doctor Nathan and had complete faith in him.

When I got to the office the tenant from the first floor was coming down the stairs and saw me. I held the door open for her. Angela Preston was an acupuncturist who had a large and flourishing practice.

"FedEx left you a package," she said. "I signed for it and got them to put it by your door, look there it is," and she pointed at a square box with the familiar blue and red lettering on it.

"Thanks very much," I said and smiled at her as she went out through the front door into the street. I stooped down to pick up the parcel. Something made me stop, and I stood up and left it where it was. I wasn't expecting anything from anybody. Maybe it was a booby trap. I let myself into my office and shut the door and rang Toby on my mobile.

"You'll think I'm becoming paranoid," I said, "but I've received a suspicious package via FedEx and I'm not expecting anything, and I've just had a warning from the bank manager that the Cottesloe Golf Club's been sold and telling me not to let Polly walk there any more, and I've been experiencing the most God-awful nightmares lately." I stopped abruptly.

"I thought you seemed a bit on edge the last time I saw you," said Toby.

That's rich coming from you, I thought, but I didn't say so.

"I'll call the local force and get them to send the bomb squad round to look at your parcel," Toby continued, "it's probably a Christmas pudding," and he rang off.

8

But it wasn't a Christmas pudding.

About a quarter of an hour after I'd spoken to Toby an unmarked car stopped outside the front door of the office and a couple of likely lads got out wearing jeans and leather jackets. They had two dogs with them on leads, an alsatian and a beagle. They rang the bell and I let them in. They showed me their police badges. I showed them the parcel, still where it lay on the floor by my door.

The beagle had a good sniff at the parcel and wagged her tail at her handler.

"That's alright," he said "it's not explosives".

Then the alsatian sniffed at the parcel and he too wagged his tail.

"It's not drugs either," said the other copper, and he picked up the parcel and held it as if judging its weight, " but it's very heavy. Do you want us to take it away or will you open it up?"

"I'll open it now," I said as he handed it to me, "and thanks a lot for coming round."

"Better safe than sorry," they said in unison and left with the dogs as quickly as they'd come. They jumped into the car, the dogs on the back seat and the coppers in front, driving off at speed without so much as a glance backwards.

I carried the box into my office. It was certainly extremely heavy for its size and I placed it on the table and carefully took off the wrapping. Inside was a corrigated cardboard box with a note carefully stuck to it with selotape, printed by a computer on plain white paper.

This geocache was found while metal detecting along the footpath on your farm buried at coordinates 51#02'36,83"N 0#18'36,64"W

I stuffed the piece of paper into my pocket and looked at the box again. There was absolutely no clue who the sender was either inside the paper wrapping or on the delivery ticket or anywhere on the box. I opened up the box and inside was a black plastic cylinder the size of a tennis ball tube. I took the lid off the tube and looked inside. There was some tissue paper scrunched up in the entrance of the tube as packing which I removed so that I could then see what looked like a lump of silver about the size and shape of a tennis ball – quite appropriate I thought – and I rolled it out on to the table. There were actually three similar silver balls and each one must have weighed about the same as a bag of flour.

I made myself a cup of tea and sat down at the table and examined the silver balls carefully. On close inspection I could see that they had been made from lots of separate pieces of metal which must have been fused together, presumably when very hot, so that they weren't perfectly round and the surface was quite rough in places.

I asked myself several questions.

Who was the sender? Why had the sender sent the package to my office and not to our home? How had the tube come to be buried on the footpath in the first place? What was the actual metal and was it at all valuable?

I decided to try and get an answer to the last question first. I put on my coat and put one of the balls in a pocket and went out of the office, locking the door behind me. I walked up West Street to Wakehursts the Jewellers and went inside and asked the woman behind the counter if Melody Wakehurst was in. She went to fetch her. I knew Melody quite well as I had bought some earrings for Polly's birthday and Melody had been very helpful and quite chatty about her business which she and her brother had inherited from her grandfather.

"How are you Tom?" she asked when she came out of the interior of the shop into the sales area.

"Fine thanks, and you?"

"We're all very well thanks. How can I help?" and she smiled in her rather charming way.

I took the silver ball out of my pocket and held it out to her.

"Can you please tell me what this is?" I asked. She took it and examined it carefully, judging its weight and turning it over and over in her hands and looking at it as a whole. Then she got her eyepiece out of her pocket and looked at the silver ball through her magnifying glass.

"Would you like to come into the back where we do the assaying, please," she said and without waiting for an answer she led the way into the inner sanctum. She placed the ball on her super-accurate digital scales. It weighed just over two kilos.

"Have you got any idea what this is?" she asked.

"Not really," I said.

"Well it's platinum," she said " and probably worth anything up to a hundred thousand pounds as scrap, depending on its purity and so on. Where did you get it from?"

I wondered how much to tell her. I decided to tell her a limited amount of the truth.

"It was found by a metal detector and it was buried on the footpath on the boundary of our smallholding," I said, "but I've got no idea how it got there."

"Well it's certainly quite a find,"said Melody "platinum is hideously expensive now and pretty rare. It's used for various industrial purposes, things like catalytic converters in cars, and electrodes, and dental equipment, as well as jewellery of course. They also use it in chemotherapy for cancer treatment. It's so expensive that there's a growing business extracting it from scrap, especially from catalytic converters, I'd say at a guess that this ball is made out of reclaimed platinum from a good number of scrapped motor cars."

Charlie Farley again, I thought. Melody looked at me.

"Would it be OK if I kept this for a while, I'd like to do some tests on it and discuss it with my father, he's a metallugist as you know, so he'd be very interested to see it? I'll give you a receipt for it if you want." and she smiled at me again. She was very persuasive.

"Oh, there's no need for that," I said, "and anyway there are two more just like it." She raised her eyebrows but didn't say any more.

"You can certainly hang on to it for a bit," I said and I went towards the showroom to leave. She walked with me to the door.

"Bye-bye," I said and went out into West Street. It was dark by now and raining quite hard. I really must get back to work, I thought, I've got such a lot to tidy up before the Christmas break. All this other stuff is very distracting.

I decided to have a coffee and a piece of cake and then go back to my office and work until it was time to go home for supper, so I went in to Costas and joined the queue. I sat at a table in the window and thought about the latest turn of events. I was miles away when I heard a familiar voice.

"Tommy, how are you?" it was Jake and Brigid. I was so pleased to see them again that I stayed on while they got a pot of tea and some biscuits and we sat together and brought each other up to date.

The sale of Jakellie Recycling had gone through and Jake's plans for his business had been given a boost by Trevor Baylis, so they were pretty chipper about everything. I didn't say much about my recent doings and after promising that we would all meet over the Christmas holiday we parted and I went back to my office.

As I walked towards my office I saw that the light was on and the curtains were drawn. My God, I thought, I'm getting so forgetful I must have failed to turn out the light. I put the key in the lock of the outside door and went into the small hallway. The door into my office was ajar and there was a metalic grinding sound coming from inside. I pushed the door open and saw two figures wearing hoodies kneeling on the floor trying to open my safe.

"Hey!" I said, "what the hell do you think....."

I got no further. There was a third person inside who was hidden behind the door and as I hurried into the room I was hit over the back of the head with something very heavy and I fell forwards on to my face and passed out.

Chapter 10

1

I came to with the most frightful headache and felt blood running down the back of my neck into my collar. Angela Preston from upstairs was leaning over me.

"Heavens," she said "are you alright? No, that's a stupid question you're obviously not at all alright. Can you understand me?" and she peered into my eyes.

"I'm OK," I said "but I don't think I could stand up for a bit," and I just sat slumped where I was.

"No," she said "don't try to do anything at all. I disturbed three men when I came in just now and they pushed past me and ran out of the front door and disappeared. I'll call the police first and they can tell us whether you need an ambulance when they get here."

She called 999 and I heard her tell the duty telephonist at the police headquarters what had happened and details of our address. Then she came back to me and tried to make me more comfortable. She brought a damp drying-up cloth and gave it to me to wipe my head and neck with.

"You'd better not have any tea or anything like that in case you need an anaesthetic, but would you like some water?"

She didn't wait for an answer but went into my kitchen and fetched a glass of water and handed it to me. I sipped it and felt marginally better. I looked around the room. Everything had been wrecked. They'd smashed my desk and emptied all the drawers out, they'd taken every book off the shelves and ripped them all in half, they'd tipped the contents of all my storage boxes and the filing cabinet on the floor in their frenzy to find whatever it was they were looking for.

They hadn't managed to open the safe but they'd had a jolly good try. It was scored with marks made by a grinder and there were several drill holes round the keyhole, it wouldn't have taken them much longer to break it open if I hadn't come back and disturbed them when I did.

There was no sign of the two platinum balls or of the container or the box anywhere that I could see.

"Shall I ring your wife?" asked Angela, "or would you rather wait for the police to come?"

"It'd be better if you rang her," I said "she'll only be alarmed if the police do."

"What's your home number?"

I told her and she dialled it. Polly answered.

"Hi there, it's Angela Preston from the suite above Tom's office," she said, "there's been a break-in and Tom's been hit on the head but he's alright. We're waiting for the police to arrive. Would you like to talk to Tom?" and she passed me the phone..

"Darling, are you OK?" asked Polly. I could hear the anxiety in her voice.

"I'm fine," I said, "everything's fine. They made a bit of a mess. I'll call you again when the police are here and let you know what time I'll be home. How's Bertie?"

"He's asleep, "said Polly, "don't drive home, just get a taxi or get the police to drive you home, and don't try to do anything until they've had a good look at you. Let everyone else do the lifting."

I felt quite emotional after she'd rung off. I sat on the floor and closed my eyes. Angela was great, she went out to the front door to wait for the police and to give me some space. I passed out again and when I came to for the second time there were several police officers in the room and a couple of paramedics bending over me.

"Now," said one of the medics "we just need to do a few tests to make sure it's alright to move you. Then we'll get you into the ambulance and take you to Haywards Heath hospital for an x-ray and some routine tests." There was no point in resisting these plans so I just let myself be carried along with the flow.

The detective inspector told me that they would put a guard outside the door and leave everything exactly as it was. The forensic people would be coming the following morning to start their work and when I felt up to it they would like to ask me some questions.

"This is robbery with violence causing grievous bodily harm at the very least," said the inspector, "it may even be attempted manslaughter. We'll have to see. First we have to catch the buggers. In the meantime the important thing is to make sure you get fit and well as soon as possible and that nothing else here is disturbed."

He looked at me. "We'll keep a watch on your home as well," said the inspector, "we don't want any more trouble. Now, you get some rest."

The paramedics decided that it was alright to move me and they put me on a stretcher and carried me to the ambulance. Angela looked on.

"Thanks for everything," I said "I don't know what might have happened if you hadn't arrived when you did."

"See you when you get back again," she said.

"I'd like to ask you a few questions tomorrow Miss," said the inspector, but I didn't catch her reply as by this time I was halfway into the ambulance.

2

I had an x-ray followed by an MRI scan. My scull was fractured in two places just above my neck. There was no damage to my brain or to any of the ligaments in my back.

"You were quite fortunate in a way," said the specialist looking at me with his pale blue eyes over his cut-off spectacles as I lay in my hospital bed, "if you'd been any shorter than you are the back of your scull might have been very severely smashed and your brain irreperably damaged, any taller and your spine could have been affected – you might have even been a paraplegic. How tall are you?"

"About six foot three or four."

"Well there you are. Have you any idea what you were hit with?" he asked.

I should think it was almost certainly one of the platinum balls, I thought, but I said "No idea I'm afraid, I never saw the guy."

"No, of course not," said the specialist, "now we'll keep you in here for a few days and keep a good eye on you. No visitors for a while except your wife. You mustn't get anxious or excited about anything. You've got a very severe concussion. I know the police want to interview you but I've forbidden that until I personally give them the go-ahead. No television or books for a day or two until your sight is completely restored, but the radio is fine. Just rest. Any questions?"

I had dozens of things I would have liked to ask him but instead I said "Not really, and thanks very much."

"All part of the service," he said and he left the room followed by his entourage.

I lay in my comfortable bed and felt pretty foolish. Fancy walking into a trap like that, after being so worried about the silly parcel. I tried to think about various things but I found it difficult to concentrate and I kept slipping in and out of sleep and finally I dozed off.

When I opened my eyes Polly was sitting by the bed looking at me.

"You look like the invisible man," she said idicating the enormous bandage I had wrapped around my head, "how are you feeling darling?" She looked fantastic.

"I'm OK," I said "I just feel such a fool."

"Well I spoke to the specialist and he told me you've actually been pretty lucky and that you should be out of here within a couple of weeks," she said.

"Good Lord," I said "two weeks in here, it seems like a life sentence". and I felt quite depressed at the thought.

"Stop being such a whinger," said Polly "you're damned lucky you weren't killed or maimed. It'll do you good to have a complete rest and Bertie and I can come and see you every day until you come home. Besides you'll soon be well enough to be able to help the police with their enquiries, and Toby and Alex can't wait to come and ask you questions too." She smiled at me. "Look, I brought you these flowers, and Frank Waller sent this beautiful orchid too. Everyone's been so concerned about you."

"Where's Bertie?" I asked.

"He's asleep in his pushchair just ouside the door, would you like to see him?" and she went outside and wheeled the pushchair into the room. There he was, fast asleep. I felt reassured and suddenly terribly tired and I drifted off to sleep again."

When I woke she'd gone, leaving a vase of beautiful friesias where I could see them.

"I'm so bloody lucky," I thought and this galvanised me into stopping feeling sorry for myself and I started to think positively again and determined to get strong and well as quickly as possible.

3

After a couple of days the specialist gave permission for the police to interview me but for not more than one hour at a time. The inspector came with a young WPC who took notes. They sat in chairs at the foot of my bed. The inspector was very quiet spoken. He started by saying that the forensic team had been over my office with a toothcomb and had come up with masses of fingerprints and some DNA samples. These were now being matched with the police database. He then asked me to take him step-by-step through my movements on the day the break-in occurred, which I did. He was particularly interested in the veiled warning from the bank manager.

When I came to the bit about opening the parcel and the typed note attached to the box he said there'd been no trace of the note.

"I put it in my pocket," I said "I expect it's still there." I rang the bell for the nurse and when she appeared I asked her if she could please bring my trousers. Sure enough the note was still in the hip pocket and I gave it to the inspector. He studied it carefully.

"Is it alright if I keep this sir?" he asked and of course I said it was fine. He handed it to the WPC and asked her to mark it exhibit A and note what it was.

"There was no sign of any of the platinum balls," said the inspector.

"No, but Melody Wakehurst has one of them in her jewellers shop," I said and I told him about my visit to Wakehursts.

"Maybe you could sign a little note to Melody Wakehurst if you don't mind," said the inspector, "asking her to release the object to me."

"Of course," I said. He dictated a note to the WPC who wrote it down and dated it and he handed it to me gravely and asked me to sign it.

"I think that's enough for a first interview," said the inspector, "we don't want to tire you out. Thank you very much for telling us everything so far. What we really need to establish is exactly what they were after."

"Obviously not just the platinum balls," I said "they got those, well two of them, anyway. I wonder what they imagined was in the safe. There's nothing of value, just notebooks and a few records."

"Thanks for that," said the inspector, "rest assured we'll do our level best to catch these felons." Then he and the WPC rose and left the room, closing the door quietly behind them. It's just like the mills of God, I thought, grinding away slowly but surely. Then I drifted off to sleep.

When I woke up there was Polly sitting by my bed again, as if by magic. She smiled at me.

"You look a lot better today," she said "have you eaten anything?"

"I had some toast and a boiled egg,"

"I brought you some grapes," she said "they're really nice ones." She went out of the room and asked for a bowl and washed the grapes and brought them back.

"Thanks very much," I said and ate one or two of them. They tasted really good, like the muscat grapes grown in hothouses.

We chatted amiably away and Polly told me that Andy and Tracy were back together again.

"It's interesting," said Polly "when I told Tracy about your accident I think it made her think what it would be like if something similar happened to Andy and she rang him up soon afterwards and told him to come back."

"I bet that was an emotional meeting," I said. It was a good result though.

"I left Bertie with Tracy today," said Polly, "she adores him and he's quite happy with her. Now he has one bottle of Aptamil a day to supplement me I can leave him with her for a few hours and she can feed him and change him. She looks after Pinky and Perky too."

It was good to get domestic news, it brought a bit of reality into the rather institutionalised life in hospital. I wondered how much longer I'd be stuck in there.

"Toby and Alex are working together again," said Polly. "Toby rang me and asked me to meet him and Alex at our office. I'd already been there after the inspector told me I could start clearing up the mess when the forensic team had finished. My God it was a mess too. It took me nearly a whole day to clear everything up. I managed to salvage all the papers and files and restored them to their right places. The desk and table were matchwood so I got some new ones."

"I took the key to the safe with me and got all your notebooks out of it and put them in a storage box in the loft of our house. Then I locked the safe again and left it empty as it was. Finally I vacuumed the carpet and floor and got a locksmith to change the lock to a deadlock Banham and put locks on all the windows too. It's ready for action when you get back."

"Wow," I said "that's great. What did Toby want?"

"Well, he was wondering what it was the thieves were looking for. It can't just have been the platinum balls because they were sitting on the table. Toby suddenly decided they were looking for the key to your safe and they ransacked the place first, then when they couldn't find the key they tackled the safe. The inspector agreed with Toby."

"It sounds like Holmes and Lestrade," I said and I laughed for the first time since I'd been knocked out. Polly giggled, "that's exactly what I thought too." She held my hand tight.

"I'd better be getting back home," she said "I expect Toby will come and see you soon. I'll be back tomorrow," and she kissed me gently and left.

The specialist came by on his rounds in the afternoon and had a good look at me. He tested my eyesight and a nurse took the bandages off and he examined the wound on the back of my head.

"Good," he said "you're making good progress. Your pupils are the same size which is an excellent sign. You can get up and do a bit of walking up and down the corridor. Just for five minutes at a time with a physio to look after you in case you feel a bit groggy. We don't want to risk you falling over. No television or books yet I'm afraid," and he went on his way with his group in train.

I heard him explaining my condition to his students as he walked away down the corridor. I heard him say "Grade three" but that was all I could catch. Oh well, I thought, as long as I'm getting better what does it matter and I lay back and relaxed.

Toby and Alex came to see me at the week-end. They'd arranged with Polly what the best time woud be so that their visit didn't coincide with hers. I'd forgotten how tall Alex was as he towered over the bed to pat my shoulder. They brought the chairs up close to my bedside so that I could relax while we chatted. Toby was never one for preamble and he launched straight into the matter in hand.

"We've done a great deal of legwork in the last ten days," he said. He took his android phone out of its sheath and switched it on and found what he was looking for and scrolled down. He looked across at Alex. "Shall I start?" asked Toby. Alex nodded.

Toby told me their story.

4

One of the things which had puzzled Toby about the Vargas affair was that it seemed impossible that Pedro aka Orlando had operated entirely alone. Toby had discussed this with Alex who had agreed with him, and they had tried to work out which other people might be involved. When I had shown Toby the ordnance map and the schedule of farms which Charlie Farley had bought over the past three years it seemed too much of a coincidence and Toby and Alex had step-by-step worked out the links.

Organised crime in the UK represents an enormous proportion of what should be part of GDP, possibly as much as £40 billion a year, and especially in three areas, arms trafficking, drug trafficking and people trafficking, the latter being mainly for prostitution. Organised crime has also increased dramatically as a result of globalisation.

Charley Farley had a wide net. Unfortunately for him, in order to operate his recycling business in West Sussex he had to be licenced by the Council and they would not issue a licence for running a scrapyard to an individual but only to a limited liability company. This meant of course that Charlie had had to register The Chaotic Scrap Metal and Recycling Company with the registrar of companies and had to be registered for VAT and for tax and file annual accounts. His head was above the parapet, but only just, and he kept the scrap part of the business pretty legitimate.

Over several years Charlie had expanded into various not-so-legitimate businesses. In so doing he had involved and corrupted quite a number of other people.

The first of these people was the head of planning at the local council. This was a man with a terrible weakness for gambling who had got himself into serious financial difficulties by losing large sums of money at the local dog track and in the casino and had only made the position worse by gambling and losing a fortune on-line. He turned up at The Chaotic Scrap Metal and Recycling Company Limited late one Friday evening with a proposition for Charlie. He would nod through an application for planning for a light industrial estate on part of the scrapyard which had road access, in return for one-third of the value of the land after planning. He reckoned this would be worth a total of six million pounds and two million would accrue to him. He would even arrange for the sale of the land to a local developer with whom he had a cosy relationship.

Charlie agreed to this proposal, provided all the paperwork and everything else was handled by the planning officer. It all went through like clockwork, including the sale of the site to the developer.

Next came the tricky little problem of how to launder the money when it came through. Charlie had struck up quite a nice relationship with his bank manager over the years and had arranged for him to acquire a Saab motor car which would normally have been way beyond his means had it not been a car which should heve been crushed under the government scheme. Charlie had crushed a different car in its place, and with a few repairs to the bodywork the Saab was re-licenced by the DVLA thanks to a backhander from Charlie to one of the people he had got to know at Swansea.

After this the bank manager couldn't do enough for Charlie who was able to open and operate several nominee savings accounts without having to jump through any of the normal regulatory hoops, and into which larger and larger sums were paid from time to time. And paid out from time to time, too.

Charlie invested his increasing wealth with great skill. He bought land mostly, remembering one of Mark Twain's better-known remarks "buy land, they ain't makin' it any more". And naturally some of the land he bought had bits and pieces which were suitable for building on and all this needed was planning consent which usually went through with very little difficulty, thus providing more funds for the nominee savings accounts and in due course for the purchase of yet more land.

And of course the planning officer also grew richer and the bank manager benefited too, he was able to buy a bigger house and went on holiday to the carribbean every winter.

After a while, and because he was open to any suggestions which would make him richer, Charlie was approached by Orlando Vargas who had found out that

Charlie owned the quarry adjoining the Cottesloe Golf Course. Vargas wondered if Charlie might be interested in selling the quarry to him. Charlie said he wasn't really interested in selling it and enquired what Vargas wanted it for. He got a rather vague reply, something to do with an environmental scheme, said Vargas, so Charlie said he'd be agreeable to renting it to him instead. Which he did.

Naturally Charlie's antennae were long enough and sensitive enough to elicit the fact that Vargas was involved in drug trafficking and also in recycling stolen goods. He soon struck up a business relationship with Vargas and was able to help him with the distribution of both drugs and stolen goods via The Chaotic Scrap Metal and Recycling Company Limited. The drugs were concealed in the hollow doors of certain large American-style motor vehicles, and the stolen goods were recycled via a Polish transport company who handled all of Charlie's international freight.

A recent enterprise was the export of small arms and weapons and ammunition to Chechnya but Charlie felt uneasy about this and decided not to continue it when the current agreement ended. Instead, he expanded the reclamation and processing of precious metals such as platinum from crushed cars through a recycling plant he had set up with a chemist in one of his more remote farmyards. This was a very dangerous process and consequently very lucrative.

The transport company also back-loaded illegal immigrants in portacabins which had been designed for the purpose and which were concealed inside the containers. They passed through all the border controls with ease thanks to backhanders in the right places. The illegal immigrants were taken on by gangmasters and in time some of them became members of the 'artful dodgers'.

Thanks to Charlie's relationship with the planning officer a blind eye was turned to the construction of the domes and the lab in the quarry. However, as soon as Vargas was arrested the planning officer issued a demolition order for the unauthorised structures to be destroyed and they were demolished immediately.

"And that brings us up to the present time," said Toby.

"Any questions?" asked Alex, and then "would it be possible to get a cup of tea d'you think, please?"

"Sure," I said and rang the bell. A nurse appeared and said hullo to Toby and Alex and went off to arrange for some tea and biscuits to be brought along. At this point Polly arrived and they got another chair for her and we all settled down to drink some tea together. Toby went through his story again for Polly. We looked at each other in amazement.

"What did Charlie want in Tom's office then?" asked Polly.

"Well he knew that Tom kept details of all his clients' affairs in his Moleskine notebooks, and he became worried that sooner or later news of some of his activities would get out. You see, Henry King mentioned to Charlie that he'd given Tom the details of the farmland purchases because he imagined that Tom did Charlie's tax returns and that it would help him with the capital gains tax section of the returns. Charlie therefore knew that Tom knew and Charlie thought Tom would have put this information in a notebook. So he sent the heavies in to get hold of the notebooks. The platinum balls were just a coincidence, and it was just luck, or bad luck for Tom, that he came back and disturbed them."

"By the way," put in Alex "the heavies are employed by a local registered and regulated security company, which is now going to have to answer some pretty awkward questions about the fact that some of their staff have been breaking and entering and causing damage to property with a view to theft, as well as trying to kill someone."

"Charlie is in custody at Lewes jail with the three heavies, and Peg is in Holloway, they're all held awaiting charges. The bank manager and the planning officer and several other of Charlie's contacts have been interviewed and warned and all their passports have been confiscated and they have to report daily to their local police station until the investigations are completed and any charges are made. Everything's in the hands of the police now, the inspector is absolutely tickled pink as you can imagine."

"So now we can all get back to normal," said Polly, "thanks so much you two for everything you've done for us, you've been fantastic." She got out of her chair and gave them each a hug.

"You'd better hurry up and get fit again soon Tom," said Toby, "so that you can come to Ellie's and my wedding." He blushed for the first time I'd ever seen him.

This caused another round of hugs and kisses and exclamations at which point the specialist entered the room with his entourage.

"I hope you're not over-exciting my patient," he said. Then he smiled for the first time since I'd met him, "actually you must be doing him some good because he's looking a lot better," he said, "but I need to be left alone with him and Mrs Verity for a while please."

"We were just about to leave anyway," said Alex, and he and Toby left the room after blowing Polly a kiss.

The specialist came to my end of the bed and asked the nurse to remove the bandages from my head again. He examined the wounds really thoroughly and then he looked into my eyes.

"How do your feel?" he asked.

"Pretty good thanks," I replied, "the headaches have gone and I'm almost walking normally again."

"Good, the physio told me the same," he said "you're getting on nicely. You may read and watch television for a bit now, but don't overdo it. I'll arrange for you to have an x-ray and another MRI scan tomorrow and then we'll decide when you can go home."

"Nice to meet you again," he said to Polly and smiled at her. Then he swept out as usual like a whale followed by his pilot fish. Polly closed the door behind him. Then she came and sat by the bed again.

"Now you're allowed to read again I've got something in the car for you," she said "I'll just go down and get it," and she slipped from the room. She returned in a few minutes with one of her big leather porfolio cases. She sat down again beside the bed and looked at me.

"Tracy was helping me yesterday," she said "and she was carrying a bundle of washing downstairs. It brushed against the picture frame hanging on the wall at the foot of the stairs, you know the one with the silhouettes of your father's family in it?"

I nodded.

"Well," she went on "the string broke and it crashed onto the floor and something broke. Tracy was terribly upset but I had a look at it and the silhouettes weren't damaged in any way although the frame was broken along one edge and the glass was smashed. I carefully cleared up the pieces of glass and took the rest of the glass out of the frame and bundled it all up and put it in the rubbish bin, then I laid the picture on the kitchen table and had a look at the mount and the backing. And I found these hidden inside the back."

She took half a dozen sheets of A3 sized paper out of her portfolio case.

"They're the mandalas your father mentioned in his notebook," she said, and she showed me each one in turn. "They're really fabulous and brilliantly drawn, Bill must have been quite artistic."

We went through the mandalas together and Polly explained them to me. She had spent a whole afternoon looking through them so as to understand exactly what they meant.

"I got your father's notebook out of the storage box in the loft, where I'd put it with all your own notebooks which I took out of the safe in the office, and I read through the last section again, you know, the bit he wrote about global warming and so on. I've brought it with me. He got the idea for the mandalas from reading a book called *The One Straw Revolution* written by Masanobu Fukuoka who was a Japanese farmer who devised a natural way of farming using no sprays or fertiliser and without even turning over the soil. I've brought that book too, it was with your Father's other books, and it's fabulous – I read it until midnight last night."

This is just the sort of task I need, I thought, how clever of Polly to think of it, and how fortunate that Tracy had knocked the picture off the wall, otherwise we'd never have found the mandalas.

Polly dug something else out of her portfolio case. It was a small oblong gift box. She handed it to me.

"Here you are, you'll need this too," she said, "it's an early Christmas present from Bertie and me."

I unwrapped the box and took out a beautiful small black fountain pen. It was a Mont Blanc ink pen with the traditional snowpeak logo on the end of the cap. There were a couple of tiny boxes of ink cartridges too.

"Now you can continue with your father's project," said Polly "his handwriting was very neat so you've got a lot to live up to."

I was absolutely thrilled with the pen. "Thanks a lot," I said and Polly leant over me so that I could kiss her properly.

"You are getting better," she said "down Rover," and she sat back on the chair again. She gave me one of her funny looks.

"You should be home in time for Christmas," she said, "and then in the new year we'll have to get the nursery ready for Bertie's little brother or sister." She grinned at me again. I looked at her enquiringly.

"Are you pregnant again?" I asked, "how fantastic."

"About three months gone," she said. This time she got into the bed with me and we hugged each other until we were disturbed by the nurse bringing me my medication. The nurse feigned mock disapproval but I could tell she was secretly pleased for us.

"I'd better get back home and relieve Tracy," said Polly, and she got out of the bed, put on her coat, kissed me goodbye and left.

5

I got home in time for Christmas which was a joyful time spent with Polly's parents in our home. We went for walks across the fields in the crisp snow and Pinky and Perky were quite mystified by the disappearance of the rabbit holes.

I gradually regained my full health and strength and thanked my lucky stars that I was quite alright and had suffered no ill-effects from the blow on my head. We never did find out how the platinum balls came to be buried on the footpath, sometimes life's mysteries are best left unsolved.

I wrote a paper on my father's research into global warming and the dangers of using up the earth's resouces. Polly drew the most exquisite set of mandalas to illustrate the paper and we submitted it for publication to the Centre for Alternative Technology at Machynlleth in Mid-Wales. The use of mandalas has since spread throughout schools and colleges to illustrate links between the components of different subjects.

Toby and Ellie were married in the Easter holidays in Worth church and spent their honeymoon in the USA so that they could attend Jeannie and Alex's wedding in Minneapolis St Paul.

Bertie's sister was born on midsummer's day, a beautiful baby girl. We decided to name her after her two grandmothers, so she was christened Camelia Evgenia.

I haven't had another nightmare since the day I was knocked out by the blow to my head. Maybe there's a moral there somewhere, about having sense knocked into you I mean, but personally I think I was just born lucky.

THE END

16573102R00136

Made in the USA
San Bernardino, CA
09 November 2014